FEELIN' KINDA PUNCHY?

His mistake, Longarm reflected as he ducked the huge, knobby fist coming right at his face, had been getting off the damn train in the first place. He should have turned around and gone back to Denver and that rich widow. Cussing himself for his own indecisiveness and Billy Vail for being so blasted smart, he threw himself forward, driving his shoulder into the belly of the man who was trying to knock his head off.

The lumberjack staggered backward on the platform of the train station. Longarm caught hold of the man's legs and heaved upward, and with a wild yell, the lumberjack went over on his back, landing heavily on the planks. Longarm almost fell, too, but he caught his balance in time to stay upright. He twisted around, waiting to see who was going to jump him next.

Instead, he saw that the ruckus was about to escalate from fisticuffs to gunplay. One of the cowboys was reaching for a Colt . . .

Includes an excerpt from

Bushwhackers

The all-new, all-action Western series from the creators of Longarm

Coming July 1997 in paperback from
Jove Books

DON'T MISS THESE
ALL-ACTION WESTERN SERIES
FROM THE BERKLEY PUBLISHING GROUP

THE GUNSMITH by J. R. Roberts
Clint Adams was a legend among lawmen, outlaws, and ladies.
They called him . . . the Gunsmith.

LONGARM by Tabor Evans
The popular long-running series about U.S. Deputy Marshal
Long—his life, his loves, his fight for justice.

SLOCUM by Jake Logan
Today's longest-running action Western. John Slocum rides a
deadly trail of hot blood and cold steel.

BUSHWHACKERS by B. J. Lanagan
An all-new series by the creators of Longarm! The rousing adventures of the most brutal gang of cutthroats ever assembled—Quantrill's Raiders. *Coming July 1997 from Jove Books*

TABOR EVANS

LONGARM

AND THE
BACKWOODS BARONESS

J

JOVE BOOKS, NEW YORK

If you purchased this book without a cover, you should be aware that
this book is stolen property. It was reported as "unsold and destroyed"
to the publisher, and neither the author nor the publisher has received
any payment for this "stripped book."

LONGARM AND THE BACKWOODS BARONESS

A Jove Book / published by arrangement with
the author

PRINTING HISTORY
Jove edition / June 1997

All rights reserved.
Copyright © 1997 by Jove Publications, Inc.
Bushwhackers excerpt copyright © 1997 by Jove Publications, Inc.
This book may not be reproduced in whole
or in part, by mimeograph or any other means,
without permission. For information address:
The Berkley Publishing Group, 200 Madison Avenue,
New York, New York 10016.

The Putnam Berkley World Wide Web site address is
http://www.berkley.com

ISBN: 0-515-12080-4

A JOVE BOOK®
Jove Books are published by The Berkley Publishing Group,
200 Madison Avenue, New York, New York 10016.
JOVE and the "J" design are trademarks
belonging to Jove Publications, Inc.

PRINTED IN THE UNITED STATES OF AMERICA

10 9 8 7 6 5 4 3 2 1

LONGARM

AND THE
BACKWOODS BARONESS

Chapter 1

Cheroot clenched between his teeth at a jaunty angle, Longarm marched through the outer office and past the openmouthed Henry, who called out futilely, "Marshal Long, just a minute—"

Longarm stalked into the office of his boss, Chief Marshal Billy Vail. The banjo clock on the office wall showed the hour as being just after nine o'clock. It was not unheard of for Longarm to arrive at the Federal Building in Denver this early in the morning, but it *was* a mite rare.

Billy Vail frowned and opened his mouth to say, "What—"

"I quit," said Longarm.

Vail gaped at him.

Longarm took the little folding wallet containing his badge and bona fides from his inside coat pocket and dropped it on the desk. He grinned at Vail. "Getting married," he said. The cheroot waggled merrily.

Vail's mostly bald head began turning pink. "Damn it, Custis!" he burst out after a moment. "What in blazes are you talking about?"

1

"The holy state of matrimony, old son. You've got a wife. You ought to know better'n anybody the joys and privileges o' wedded bliss."

"But you . . . you . . ." Vail sputtered. "Hell, Longarm, you know the old saying. You're already getting the milk for free, so why buy the—"

Longarm held up a hand, palm out. "Don't say it, Billy. I've seen the error of my ways. It's time I made an honest woman out of that friendly widow who's been keeping company with me."

Vail put his hands on his desk and levered himself to his feet. "That friendly *rich* widow?"

"Billy, you wound me deeply!" Longarm exclaimed, placing a hand over his heart. "The fact that she just picked up a tidy little dividend from some of her investments has got nothing to do with my decision."

With a snort, Vail shook his head. "To think that I'd lose my best deputy to something so venal as greed." He picked up a folder from his desk and shook it at Longarm. "And just when I was about to give you a new assignment too!"

Almost against his will, Longarm found his eyes drawn to the folder in Vail's hand. "New assignment?" he heard himself repeating.

"That's right. Figured you could handle it better than any of my other men."

"Is that so?" Longarm sat down in the leather chair in front of Vail's desk and cocked his right foot on his left knee. "I reckon it wouldn't hurt anything to listen to the details."

"Oh, no," Vail said, looking aghast. "You're not a federal officer anymore, remember? You resigned, turned in your badge." He sank into his chair and gestured to the wallet Longarm had tossed so casually onto the desk a few minutes earlier. "I'll just have Henry send word for one of the other deputies to come in. Mike Davis, maybe. He hasn't had an assignment in a while."

"Davis!" repeated Longarm. "The reason Davis ain't had an assignment lately is 'cause he couldn't find his ass with both hands!"

"I imagine he can handle this," Vail said confidently. "Of

course, people *are* getting killed, and the government's got quite a bit of money riding on things, so I hope he can get this mess untangled kind of quick-like.''

"Damn it, Billy," Longarm said as he leaned forward and reached for the folder on Vail's desk. "At least let me take a look at the paperwork. Maybe I could suggest somebody—"

"Get your hands off that folder, Long." Billy Vail's voice was as cold as the snow and ice that still capped the peaks of the Front Range, despite the fact that it was summer. "That's the property of the United States Justice Department, and like I said, it's none of your business anymore."

"But Billy . . .''

Vail leaned back in his chair and folded his hands across his ample middle. "Why, if you were to pick up that folder and read the report inside, I'd have to assume that you were rescinding your resignation and wanted to be considered for the assignment. In that case, you'd have to pick up your badge and your identification papers too."

For a long moment, Longarm stared across the desk at his former boss. Then he sighed and stubbed out his cheroot in Vail's ashtray. With his right hand he reached for the folder, while with the left he scooped up the wallet containing his badge. "You're a hard-hearted son of a bitch, you know that?" he muttered.

"Damn straight." As Longarm opened the folder, Vail added, "Looks like you're going back to timber country."

"Yeah. Looks like." Longarm started reading.

A half hour later, as he strode out of the Federal Building with travel vouchers and a copy of the report folded up in his coat pocket, he lit another cheroot and took a deep drag on it. Then he turned and looked through the crystal-clear air at the mountains and felt, as he always did, the irresistible pull of faraway places and new challenges. Once again, he was free to answer that siren's call.

Grinning to himself, Longarm said quietly, "Much obliged, Billy. Reckon I must've been out of my head, 'cause I pert' near made a mighty big mistake."

• • •

His mistake, Longarm reflected as he ducked the huge, knobby fist coming right at his face, had been getting off the damn train in the first place. He should have turned around and gone back to Denver and that rich widow. Cussing himself for his own indecisiveness and Billy Vail for being so blasted smart, he threw himself forward, driving his shoulder into the belly of the man who was trying to knock his head off.

The lumberjack staggered backward on the platform of the train station. Longarm caught hold of the man's legs and heaved upward, and with a wild yell the lumberjack went over on his back, landing heavily on the planks. Longarm almost fell too, but he caught his balance in time to stay upright. He twisted around, waiting to see who was going to jump him next.

Instead, he saw that the ruckus was about to escalate from fisticuffs to gunplay. One of the cowboys was reaching for a Colt.

Longarm stepped forward quickly, palming out his own .44 from the cross-draw rig on his left hip. The cowboy who figured to start shooting had his back half-turned to Longarm, so Longarm was able to take him unawares and clout him on the skull. The puncher's high-crowned hat absorbed most of the blow's force, just as Longarm intended, but it was still enough to drive him to his knees and make the half-drawn gun slip from his fingers.

Since he already had his own Colt in his hand, Longarm put a round into the roof that extended out over the platform. The roar of the gun made the brawlers scattered around the platform stop what they were doing. In some cases, they froze with fists cocked back in readiness for another punch.

"That's enough, damn it!" shouted Longarm. "Next fella who throws a punch is liable to be hobbling for the rest of his life from a bullet through the leg!"

One of the lumberjacks glowered at him and demanded, "Who ___ ___ ll're you, mister?"

___ gives you the right to go mixin' in with our ___ ed one of the cowboys.

___ vho just waded into a fight that ain't any of ___ d Longarm, preferring not to flash his badge

4

and reveal his true identity this early in the case, "but when you go to trying to knock my head off, I'll *make* it my business."

"Nobody figured to hurt you, mister," said one of the lumberjacks, rubbing a sore jaw. He pointed across the platform, where the cowboys were regrouping. "It's them damn cow nurses who caused all the trouble!"

"That's a damn lie!" shot back one of the cowboys. "It was you ax-swingin' bastards who bulled in where you weren't wanted!"

"If it wasn't for us, this whole state would go belly-up! You can't raise cattle in the mountains!"

"The hell you say! We can raise cattle any damn place we want!"

Longarm sighed tiredly. It looked like he might have stepped right into one of the sources of the trouble he was here to investigate.

Several days had passed since he had left Denver. Several days spent in railroad cars that rattled more and shook more the closer he came to his destination, days spent breathing air that grew more and more cinder-clogged. Finally, the narrow-gauge spur line that ran up here into the foothills of the Cascade Mountains had deposited him in a place called Timber City, and when he had stepped off the train, he had found himself smack-dab in the middle of a melee between lumberjacks in lace-up boots, khaki pants, and red-checked shirts and cowboys in chaps and Stetsons and cowhide vests. To save his own hide, he had been forced to drop his warbag, saddle, and rifle and defend himself.

The combatants had grudgingly stopped fighting. The lumberjacks formed a sullen group on one side of the train station's platform, the cowboys an equally petulant knot of rannies on the other side. Longarm looked at both groups in disgust and slid his revolver back into its holster. He turned back to the spot where he had dropped his gear and picked it up again.

"You can beat the hell out of each other when I'm gone," he said. "I don't give a damn either way."

He stalked across the platform and into the lobby of the

depot. The railroad clerk had come out from behind his ticket counter so that he could watch the brawl through the windows. Now he retreated behind the counter as Longarm came toward him.

"Yes, sir, what can I do for you?" the man asked.

Longarm set his saddle down and jerked a thumb over his shoulder at the platform behind him. "What in blazes was that ruckus about?"

The clerk sighed and shook his head. "They don't need a reason. Whenever those loggers from McEntire's camp are anywhere around the punchers from the Diamond K, a fight breaks out, just like clockwork."

"They don't get along, huh?"

"That's putting it mildly, Mister . . . ?"

"Long, Custis Long." Longarm had never been to Timber City before, so he didn't see any reason not to use his real name. If he ran into anybody he had been responsible for throwing in jail in the past, they would recognize him as much by his tall, rangy build and longhorn mustache as they would by his name. He went on. "I reckon the Diamond K must be one of the spreads hereabouts."

"That's right. It's about ten miles north of here, spread out along the foothills at the base of the Cascades. And that's about where the McEntire lumber camp is, only it's up higher in the mountains."

Longarm nodded, thankful for the fact that most pencil pushers like this gent were the talkative sort. "Well, I'll be sure not to get in the middle of those two bunches again. A fella could get killed, happen he wasn't careful."

The clerk looked solemn. "Several men have been killed already, I'm afraid. All by accident . . . or so the story goes."

"That so?"

"Yes, I think—" The clerk stopped abruptly. He grinned sheepishly. "But I'm not paid to think, just to sell tickets. Too much gossip might make people afraid to come to Timber City, and then the railroad wouldn't make as much money, would it?"

"Reckon not," said Longarm, disappointed that the man had decided to stop talking about the local troubles. Longarm

6

couldn't press him on the matter, though, not without appearing overly curious—and that was something he didn't want to do just yet. He changed the subject by asking, "There a good hotel here in town?"

"Certainly. The Ponderosa House, just down the street. You can't miss it."

"Much obliged," said Longarm as he picked up his saddle again. He turned, then asked over his shoulder, "What about a livery stable? I might need to rent a horse."

"Right next to the hotel. Affiliated with it, in fact. They'll take good care of you."

"Thanks."

Longarm left the station before the clerk could start asking any questions of his own, like who Longarm was and what he was doing there in Timber City. Longarm planned to keep that to himself for the time being, at least until he'd had a chance to talk to McEntire and find out more about the trouble that had been plaguing the timber company, costing the lives of several loggers in the process. From what he had seen so far, he had some pretty likely culprits in those Diamond K punchers.

Those same cowhands came around the corner of the building, and Longarm cast a quick glance around for the lumberjacks, figuring there was going to be more trouble. The timber-cutters had disappeared, however, forestalling another ruckus.

And being escorted by the cowboys was a mighty pretty young woman, Longarm noted. She was well-dressed in a bottle-green traveling outfit, and had what appeared to be long red hair tucked up and pinned in a bun under her stylish hat. A couple of the cowboys were carrying valises, and Longarm noticed a spring wagon parked near the depot. He wasn't surprised when the whole bunch headed toward the wagon.

There was a footstep behind him, and he glanced around to see that the ticket clerk had followed him out onto the porch. "Deserting your wicket, ain't you?" asked Longarm.

"Business is slack right now," replied the clerk with a shrug. "Besides, I wanted a look at Molly Kinsman. She's been gone to school back East for a while, and I'd heard she

7

had changed a heap." He let out a low whistle of admiration as he watched the young woman being helped into the spring wagon by one of the punchers. "Changed for the better too, she did."

"Kinsman," Longarm mused. "Her daddy must own the Diamond K."

"That's right. Matt Kinsman was one of the first ranchers in these parts. Still has one of the biggest and best spreads." The clerk looked over at Longarm and added curiously, "Say, you're just full of questions, aren't you, mister?"

That was just the reaction Longarm had hoped to avoid by leaving the station when he had. He hadn't counted on the blasted clerk following him. Still, he had gotten some more information out of the fellow, who flapped his gums like he hadn't seen another human being in a month of Sundays and was desperate to talk.

Longarm shrugged casually. "I like to know what's going on in a place when I come to visit," he said. "Been a while since I've had a riding job. Might just pay a visit to this fella Kinsman."

The clerk looked askance at him. "You don't look much like a cowboy in that town suit."

"Oh, these are just my go-to-meetin' duds. My range clothes are in my warbag."

The spring wagon from the Diamond K rattled away as Longarm made his excuses to the clerk. Several of the cowboys were riding on the wagon with the young woman; the rest of the bunch trailed it on horseback.

"Don't know if Matt Kinsman's hiring or not," said the clerk, rubbing his jaw in thought. "Like I told you, he's still got a good spread, but times are a little tight for him right now. He lost some cows to rustlers not long ago, then lost some more when he had a well go bad. Course, to hear Kinsman tell it, somebody poisoned that well, but I can't think of anybody around here who'd do a low-down thing like that."

What about those lumberjacks? Longarm asked himself. There was bad blood between the two groups; he had caught on to that fact within moments of arriving there in Timber City. If he was going to lean toward the Diamond K punchers

8

as likely suspects in the trouble to hit the McEntire lumber camp, wasn't it just as fair to think that maybe the lumberjacks had something to do with Kinsman's problems?

No matter how you looked at it, the whole thing had the makings of a pure-dee mess. And he was going to have to sort it out as quickly as he could, because Uncle Sam had money riding on the McEntire Timber Company.

"I'll probably talk to Kinsman anyway, can't hurt," Longarm commented to the clerk. Then, with another casual wave, he set off down the street toward the hotel. This time, the clerk didn't follow, as Longarm saw with a glance behind him, and he was grateful for that.

He couldn't dispute that the Ponderosa House was probably the best hotel in Timber City, but that didn't mean it was fancy, not by any stretch of the imagination. It was a three-story frame structure built of whitewashed pine. There was no porch. The front door opened directly onto the street, which was still muddy in places from some recent rains. Longarm was able to avoid the worst of the mud, so he didn't track any into the lobby when he entered the hotel.

That didn't stop the clerk behind the desk from pointing to a sign beside the door and growling, "Can't you read, mister?"

Longarm looked back at the sign, which read, "PLEASE WIPE YOUR FEET." He squinted and said, "Maybe I can make it out. It says . . . lemme see . . . the fella with the money is generally right, and the hired help shouldn't chase him off."

The clerk flushed angrily, but he said, "Sorry, mister. I'm just tired of sweepin' dried mud out of here. What can I do for you?"

"Need a room," said Longarm.

"For how long?"

"Don't rightly know. Two or three days, more'n likely, maybe longer."

The clerk turned the register around so that it faced Longarm. "Come to Timber City on business?"

"Mostly just seeing the country." Longarm grinned. "But I wouldn't mind combining a little business with pleasure, if the right opportunity was to come along.'' He scrawled his name on the register.

The clerk was good at reading upside down, probably from long practice. ''What line of business're you in, Mr. Long?''

''Little o' this, little o' that,'' Longarm said, being deliberately vague. He had hinted to the ticket clerk over at the depot that he was a cowboy. Maybe he should have intimated to this fella that he was in the timber business. Keeping folks off balance was generally a good idea, especially in a case with as many unanswered questions as this one. Until his investigation had shed some light on things, it usually paid to keep everybody else in the dark too.

''Well, if there's anything we here at the Ponderosa House can do for you, you just let us know.'' The clerk took a key from the board behind him and slid it across the desk. ''You'll be in Number Eighteen. Go to the top of the stairs and down the hall. Room's at the far end, on the left.''

That would put it at the back of the hotel. ''Best you've got?'' asked Longarm.

The clerk shrugged. ''This town's a busy place, in case you hadn't noticed.''

Longarm had noticed. The streets of Timber City were full of wagons and buckboards and horsebackers. Though it was named for the heavily wooded slopes of the Cascades to the west, the town was also the supply center for all the ranches in the area, which were also flourishing. That was what they called the best of both worlds, Longarm supposed.

But right now, they appeared to be worlds in collision, and that could cause a heap of damage unless someone intervened.

That was his job, to plunk himself right down between two incredible forces rushing head-on at each other—

And try not to get crushed in the process.

10

Chapter 2

The ticket clerk at the train station proved to be right about the livery stable. Longarm was able to rent a long-legged roan gelding for a price that wasn't too outrageous, and since he had his own saddle, he didn't have to pay extra to have the livery supply one.

The hostler was a stove-up old cowboy, which came as no surprise. Hostlers seemed to come in only two varieties, Longarm reflected: geezers like this one or wet-behind-the-ears kids. The old-timer's name was Charley Dodge, not that Longarm asked. The old fellow volunteered it as Longarm was saddling the roan.

"And you'd be . . . ?"

"Name's Custis," Longarm supplied.

"Well, howdy do, Mr. Custis. What brings you to Timber City?"

"Looking around the country," said Longarm. "Thought I'd get me a job. Maybe riding for one of the ranches hereabouts, or even cutting down trees."

Charley shook his head solemnly. "You don't want to cut

11

down trees for a livin'. 'Taint honorable. Man like you needs a ridin' job.''

Longarm had changed into denim pants and a butternut shirt with a dark brown vest over it. He wore the vest so he would have a place to keep his pocket watch and the deadly little derringer that served as a fob on the other end of the watch's chain. He had to admit that he looked more like a cowboy than a lumberjack.

"You look like you've pushed a few cows in your day," he said to the old hostler as he finished tightening the cinch on the saddle.

Charley slapped his thigh. "Still would be if a bull hadn't busted this here leg of mine in two places."

"Ever ride for the Diamond K? I hear that's one of the best spreads around here."

"Matt Kinsman's ranch? Sure, I rode for ol' Matt for a while."

"What sort of gent is he?" asked Longarm.

"Hard as granite. You don't never want to cross him. But I reckon he's fair. Boys who ride for his brand seem to swear by him."

"Maybe I'll ride out and see him."

"If'n you do, tell him ol' Charley Dodge says howdy do. He'll remember me. Kinsman's riders are loyal to him, 'cause he's loyal to them."

Longarm swung up into the saddle. "Much obliged. Be seein' you, Charley."

He rode out through the big double doors of the stable and turned the horse to the left, which pointed him north. According to the talkative clerk at the depot, both Matt Kinsman's ranch and the McEntire Timber Company's camp were about ten miles north of town. It was only early afternoon; he would have plenty of time to pay a visit to the lumber camp and let McEntire know he was on the scene. Then he could ride on to Kinsman's place and maybe get there around supper time. Odds were, he would be invited to join the Kinsman family for the evening meal. That would give him the chance to do some more unobtrusive digging.

One thing you could say for this country—it was mighty

12

pretty. Steep-sided mountains covered with pines shouldered their way into the sky, and the blue of the heavens contrasted with the dark green of the forests to create a restful picture. Throw in some billows of white clouds floating above the snow-crested peaks in the distance, add the crisp, clean, pine-scented air and the murmur of crystal-clear, ice-cold streams running through the valleys, and you had some downright beautiful scenery. Longarm took deep breaths and kept his eyes wide open as he rode, trying to drink it all in.

He was unsure how far he had ridden from town when he heard some new sounds in the distance, blending with the bird calls and the rustling of small animals closer by. A steady *thunk-thunk-thunk* and the muttering of an engine, counter-pointed by the faint, echoing shouts of men. Loggers at work, he thought, the axes biting deeply into the flesh of the trees, donkey engines hauling the fallen logs to a stream where they could be fastened into a boom, warning shouts of "Timberrrr!" as the great giants of the forest toppled. Each of the industries that were spreading throughout the West had their own distinctive sounds, never to be forgotten once they had been heard . . . and Longarm had heard damn near all of them at one time or another.

When he turned onto a side trail that led up into the mountains a few minutes later, he heard another, all-too-familiar sound: the metallic clatter of a Winchester's lever action being worked.

"Hold it, mister!" rang a shout from a nearby stand of trees. The growth was thick and provided good cover for the rifle-man concealed there. As Longarm reined in, he saw the blued-steel snout of a Winchester poking through the green pine boughs.

Longarm sat still in the saddle, making no move except to half-raise his hands, even though the rifleman hadn't told him to put 'em up. He didn't want to give the man any excuse for an itchy trigger finger. "I'm not looking for trouble," he called out.

"You're a cowboy, aren't you?" The angry, accusing words shot out from the trees.

"Not right at the moment, no, I ain't," said Longarm. "I

13

won't lie to you, I did some cowboying when I came out West after the Late Unpleasantness, but I ain't pushed steers in a long time.''

"Fought in the war, did you?"

"Yep, but don't ask me on which side, 'cause I tend to disremember."

A chuckle came from the brush, but it wasn't necessarily a friendly sound. "Me too. What's your business out here?"

"I'm looking for the McEntire lumber camp. Got business with the boss there."

"Is that so?" There was a crackle of branches being parted, and the rifleman stepped out of his hiding place. He was in his thirties, Longarm judged, and his lace-up boots and checkered shirt marked him as a lumberjack, though at the moment he was wielding a Winchester instead of an ax. He gestured curtly with the barrel of the rifle and went on. "I work for McEntire Timber. Best tell me what your business is."

Longarm shook his head. "Nope. I'll only talk to your boss."

The lumberjack's face purpled with anger. Given all the trouble the timber company had experienced recently, it made sense that they had posted guards. And the way Longarm was dressed, he wasn't surprised that this sentry had taken him for a cowboy, which made him a natural enemy so far as this lumberjack knew. What with all the tension between the two groups, it didn't take much of a stretch of the imagination to see that this fella might just blast him out of the saddle and be done with it.

Reading the menace in the lumberjack's eyes, Longarm said quietly, "You might want to think twice about what you're considering, old son. Happens that I'm a lawman, a deputy United States marshal, and you don't want to go shooting federal officers."

The lumberjack frowned. "A marshal? You sure?"

"I can show you my badge, if you don't mind me reaching into my vest pocket."

"Make it slow and easy," the man warned.

Longarm was reaching for the wallet containing his identification when a wagon came around a bend in the trail up

14

ahead. It was moving fairly fast, and the man sitting beside the driver, as well as the handful of men in the back of the wagon, were all well armed. Bristling with rifles, in fact. They were all timber-cutters, like the man who had confronted Longarm.

The sentry must have signaled somebody else when he spotted a stranger in range clothes, Longarm figured, probably by flashing a mirror at a guard post higher on the mountain. That had brought the whole wagon load of guards rushing down in case Longarm proved to be the vanguard of an attack. These lumberjacks really were worried about more trouble coming their way.

The man driving the wagon, though somewhat older than his companions, was dressed like them. His lined, weathered features and the iron-gray hair on his head set him apart from the younger men. Despite his age, his forearms were bulky with muscle under the rolled-up sleeves of his shirt, and his rangy build hinted at enough power and stamina to keep chopping down trees all day, and all night too if need be. He brought the vehicle to a halt about twenty feet away from Longarm and called out to the sentry, "Who's this, Andy?"

"Says he's a badge-toter, Mr. Flint," replied the guard. "A deputy United States marshal."

The man called Flint raised bushy gray eyebrows in surprise. "Is that so?"

Longarm finished sliding his identification out of his inside vest pocket. He opened the wallet and held it up so that the afternoon sunlight glinted off the badge pinned inside. "Name's Long, Custis Long," he said.

Flint dropped down from the wagon seat and stalked toward Longarm, squinting up at the badge as he came alongside the roan. He grunted. "Looks all right," he admitted. "I knew the government promised the boss some help. Looks like you're it."

"Reckon I am," said Longarm dryly.

Flint stuck up a hand. "Jared Flint. I'm the foreman of the McEntire timber operation. I can take you up to the headquarters camp if you'd like."

"That's what I'm here for, Mr. Flint."

"I'll turn the wagon around and you can follow us up to the guard post. I can pick up a horse there and take you the rest of the way."

"Much obliged."

Flint grunted again. He wasn't the friendliest fella Longarm had ever run across, but the hostility Longarm had sensed initially seemed to have disappeared. All of the lumberjacks had relaxed since finding out he was a lawman and not some cowhand from the Diamond K bent on mischief.

It took only a few minutes to reach the shack that served as a guard post. Flint swung up onto the back of one of the saddle horses tied there and led Longarm up the twisting trail that writhed back and forth like a snake across the heavily timbered face of the mountain. Longarm judged that half an hour had gone by when they came in sight of the lumber camp.

It was like a small settlement, complete with a store, a mess hall, and a square little building with a cross on top of it that Longarm took to be a chapel. A good-sized creek ran past the camp, and perched on the near bank was a sawmill built of wood and tin. Next to the mill was an impressive-looking log cabin with a porch built onto the front of it. Beyond the mess hall were several long, low buildings that Longarm took to be barracks where the loggers slept.

Jared Flint pointed his mount toward the log cabin. Longarm followed, looking at the sawmill and seeing smoke rising from a tin stack on top of the roof. He could hear the chattering roar of a steam engine coming from inside the building, along with the high-pitched whine of a saw. No one was moving around the camp except a bald-headed, gray-aproned cook who was pouring out a bucket of dishwater next to the mess hall, but the sawmill was obviously in operation. The rest of the loggers were higher on the mountain, felling trees and hauling them to the creek so that they could be floated down to the mill.

As Longarm and Flint drew rein in front of the cabin, a woman stepped out onto the porch, taking Longarm by surprise. It wasn't unheard of to find a woman in a logging camp; some of them worked as cooks or washerwomen, and some camps even had schoolmarms to teach the children of married loggers who brought their families to the camp with them. That didn't appear to be the case here, since Longarm hadn't seen a schoolhouse or any smaller cabins where families could stay. The barracks seemed to indicate that all the McEntire loggers were either single or temporarily batching it.

The woman on the porch was sure something to look at, though. Tall and in her early thirties, Longarm judged, with thick, lustrous dark hair gathered at the back of her head in a loose bun. She wore a simple, dark gray dress that tried but failed in its attempt to conceal the lushness of her figure. Her hazel eyes were alert and intelligent as they looked curiously at Longarm.

"Who is this, Mr. Flint?" she asked in a clear voice that reminded Longarm of those mountain streams such as the one behind the cabin.

Longarm didn't wait for the foreman to introduce him. He tugged on the brim of his snuff-brown Stetson and said, "Deputy U.S. Marshal Custis Long, ma'am."

She took a deep breath that lifted the proud thrust of her bosom even more. "We've been expecting you, Marshal," she said. "Are you alone?"

"Yes, ma'am."

A slight frown creased her forehead. "I wish you'd brought some more men with you. You're liable to need them."

"Well, I'll do what I can to help," Longarm said modestly. "And you'd be . . . ?"

"I'm Aurora McEntire. This is my camp."

Now it was Longarm's turn to frown. The report he had read in Billy Vail's office had included complaints of trouble from the owner of the lumber operation, A. J. McEntire. Longarm sure as hell hadn't expected that to turn out to be a woman.

Still, if that was the situation he had to deal with, so be it. He swung down from the saddle and flipped the horse's reins over a hitch rack in front of the cabin. As Longarm stepped up onto the porch, Jared Flint said, "I'll be getting back to work now, ma'am."

Aurora McEntire's voice was sharp as she said, "No, Mr. Flint, I want you to stay while I talk with Marshal Long. You

17

know as much about the trouble we've been having as I do.''

Flint shrugged and dismounted, following Longarm up onto the porch. Aurora turned and led them into the cabin.

The high-ceilinged room in which Longarm found himself was surprising well appointed for being in a lumber camp. A thick rug was spread out on the puncheon floor. To the right was a fireplace with an overstuffed divan in front of it, to the left a big hardwood table that evidently served not only for meals but also as a desk for Aurora McEntire. Papers were spread out on one end of it where a chair was drawn up to the table. A door on the other side of the table led into what were probably Aurora's sleeping quarters. The windows had oilcloth in them instead of glass, but they were covered with fancy curtains anyway.

Aurora gestured at the table and said, "Have a seat, Marshal Long. You too, Mr. Flint. Would you like a drink, Marshal?"

Longarm smiled. "Don't reckon you'd have any Maryland rye?"

Aurora returned the smile and shook her head. "I'm afraid not. I can offer you some brandy, or there's a pot of coffee on the stove."

"Coffee'll do fine," Longarm told her. "Maybe with a dollop of that brandy in it, if it's not too much trouble."

"No trouble at all," she assured him. "Mr. Flint?"

"No, thank you, ma'am," replied the foreman. He looked as if the very idea of his boss offering him a drink made him uncomfortable, even if she *was* a woman.

Aurora went to the cast-iron stove in the corner and poured two cups of coffee from the pot. She took a bottle from a cabinet and added a splash of brandy to each cup, then brought them over to the table. Longarm had liked her on sight, and the fact that she took brandy in her coffee made him admire her that much more. She was utterly feminine, yet clearly she didn't go in for the pretenses that a lot of women did. Of course, for a woman to run a lumber camp and be successful at it, she would have to be pretty forthright.

She sipped her coffee and then said, "In case you're wondering, Marshal, my late husband founded the McEntire Timber Company. When Angus passed away a couple of years ago, I took over the business."

"So you're the A. J. McEntire who got in touch with the Justice Department and asked for help with your troubles here," said Longarm.

"That's right. I don't hide the fact that I'm a woman, but I don't always advertise it either. In this case, I don't think it would have mattered. The government has a stake in our problems. Our contract to supply lumber for government construction projects involves hundreds of thousands of dollars, and unnecessary delays on delivery cost not only the McEntire Timber Company, they cost the federal treasury as well."

"That's why I'm here," Longarm pointed out. He lifted the cup to his lips. The coffee was black and strong, just the way he liked it, with a little added wallop from the brandy.

Aurora looked down at the table. "Like I said, I wish they had sent more than one man. No offense, Marshal Long, but it may take quite a bit of manpower to wipe out those troublemaking ranchers."

Longarm leaned back in his chair and held up a hand. "Hold on a minute, ma'am. Let's eat this apple one bite at a time. Nobody said anything about wiping out anybody."

"It was just a . . . figure of speech," said Aurora, shaking her head. "I suppose I'm just so frustrated by all the trouble . . ."

Jared Flint spoke up. "If you ask me, wiping 'em out is a good idea, Miz McEntire. Then they wouldn't kill any more honest loggers."

Longarm ignored the angry tone of the foreman's voice. He drank a little more coffee, then said to Aurora, "Tell me exactly what all has happened."

She sighed. "It started when a pulley rope snapped and dropped one of our toppers about a hundred and fifty feet. The poor boy never regained consciousness before he died. Accidents happen, of course, but when we checked the rope that broke, it looked like it had been partially cut."

"That'd make it murder, all right," admitted Longarm.

"A few days later, an ax blade flew off its handle while it was being swung and hit another cutter in the leg. The rest of

19

the crew kept him from bleeding to death, but he'll never be able to work again. The injury was so bad he lost the use of his leg.''

"Damn near cut it off," muttered Flint.

"Again it was something that could have been an accident," Aurora went on, "but I think the head of that ax was deliberately loosened."

"Any way of proving it?" asked Longarm.

Aurora shook her head. "Not really. The axes are kept in the tool shed at the back of the mess hall, so anybody could have gotten in there fairly easily. After that, I ordered that all axes be checked first thing in the morning before the men go to work."

"Seems like a sensible precaution," said Longarm. "What else?"

"Someone tried to burn down the mill. We were just lucky that Mr. Flint saw the flames in time to rouse the men, and they were able to put out the blaze before it did too much damage. If the mill had been destroyed, that would have been a catastrophe.''

"Again, you're sure it was deliberate?"

Flint said, "I saw some bastard—beggin' your pardon, ma'am—in a cowboy hat skulking around over there just after dusk that day, and not five minutes later, flames were shooting up along the wall. After we formed a bucket brigade and put out the fire, you could still smell the kerosene that somebody had splashed around."

That was pretty damning evidence, thought Longarm, but not completely conclusive. "Anything else?" he asked.

"The worst loss of life occurred a couple of weeks ago," said Aurora. "One of the donkey engines we use to haul logs down to the stream overheated and blew up. Four men working on the boom next to the bank were killed in the explosion. The safety valve had been tied closed. We know that because we found part of it with some charred cord still attached to it.''

"Anything happen since then?"

"No . . . but it's only a matter of time until Kinsman and his men try again."

Longarm rasped a thumbnail along the line of his jaw and frowned in thought. "I heard about Matt Kinsman in Timber City. Why would he or any other rancher want to put you out of business?"

Aurora waved a slender hand in disgust. "They say that what we're doing is going to ruin the range further down the mountains and in the foothills. They say that without the trees we're cutting down to slow it down, the runoff from the rains will wash away the best soil and foul their water supply."

"Any truth to that?" asked Longarm.

Aurora hesitated, then said, "In some cases, there might be. Some logging operations clear-cut the trees and don't leave anything behind when they're through. But the McEntire Timber Company doesn't. Angus learned when he was a young man in Scotland how to cut selectively so that the forest isn't ruined, and I've carried on with that as best I can." Her voice became more fervent as she added, "I intend for my descendants to still be logging on these slopes a hundred years from now."

That was an admirable goal, thought Longarm, but he wasn't sure how sincere she was about it. He asked, "Has anybody ever bothered explaining this to Kinsman? Maybe he'd listen to reason."

Flint snorted in contempt. "That stiff-necked bastard would never believe anything good about loggers." This time he didn't bother apologizing for his language.

"I told Kinsman he was wrong about us," said Aurora, "and he told me the only reason he wouldn't call me a liar to my face is because I'm a woman." She shook her head. "He thinks what he wants to think, Marshal, and won't be budged by explanations."

"Well, I ain't saying I'm convinced he's to blame for your troubles, but if he is, he can't go around killing people because of some mistaken notion he's got."

Flint took a watch from the pocket of his trousers and flipped it open. As he closed it, he scraped his chair back. "I got to be getting back to the men, Miz McEntire. You and the marshal need me anymore?"

"No, you go ahead, Mr. Flint. Thank you for helping me

explain to Marshal Long about what's been happening.''

Flint looked hard at Longarm. ''If you want to put a stop to this, Marshal, you're liable to have to put Kinsman in jail. Either that, or kill him. And if you don't—''

''That's enough, Mr. Flint,'' said Aurora sharply.

Flint stood there for a second, weathered face hard with anger. Then he nodded curtly and turned toward the door. When he had stalked out of the cabin, Aurora said to Longarm, ''I'm sorry, Marshal. My foreman isn't normally so hotheaded. He's just tired of the men facing unnecessary risks. There are already enough dangers that go with the job of logging.''

''Yes, ma'am, that's true enough,'' agreed Longarm. He put his hands flat on the table and pushed himself to his feet. ''Sounds to me like the first thing I need to do is make sure Kinsman's really to blame for that sabotage. If he is, he'll answer for it.''

Aurora stood up as well and went to the door of the cabin with him. As they stepped out onto the porch, she said, ''Kinsman has to be behind it. No one else has any reason, even a mistaken one, to hate us that much.''

Longarm nodded. What she said made sense, all right, but there was still a little matter of proof. He took a cheroot from his vest pocket and slid it unlit into his mouth. Around it he said, ''I'll try to ride back out here tomorrow, let you know what I've found out—''

He broke off as a startled yell came from near the mess hall. As Longarm looked up, he saw the bald-headed old cook start to run toward them. The man was waving toward the creek and yelling something, but Longarm couldn't make out the words over the rumble of the sawmill's engine and the screech of the saw as it bit through the timber being fed to it. He muttered, ''What in blazes?''

''Boom!'' shouted the cook, coming closer. ''Look out . . . boom!''

Longarm glanced over at Aurora McEntire and saw her eyes widening in fear.

Then the loudest crash he had ever heard in his life sounded right behind them.

Chapter 3

Longarm was moving almost before the thunderous roar of destruction began to assault his ears. His hand shot out and clamped around Aurora McEntire's arm, and he dove forward off the porch, taking her with him. He barely heard her scream over the noise, which was now taking on a grinding quality. When the two of them hit the ground, Longarm wrapped his arms around her and kept rolling.

He came to a stop some ten feet away from the spot where they had landed. When he lifted his head and looked back at that spot, he saw several beams from the ceiling that had been over the porch now lying there. The porch had collapsed, like the cabin behind it. Through the rubble, Longarm could see the ends of several huge logs jutting up out of the creek. It was those logs, tied together into a boom, that had been carried along the fast-moving stream to crash into the cabin.

As Longarm sat up, Aurora pushed herself onto her elbows beside him and stared in horror at what remained of the cabin. "M-my God!" she exclaimed. "What happened?"

Before Longarm could answer, the cook pounded up to

them and yelped, "Miz McEntire! Miz McEntire! Are you all right?"

"I'm fine, Eli," she assured him as she sat up and ran her fingers through her hair, which had come loose from its bun and was now dotted with splinters and sawdust. "Thanks to Marshal Long, the porch roof didn't fall on us."

"Pure dumb luck," Longarm told her. "I heard all hell breaking loose behind us and just wanted to get out of there as fast as I could."

"Don't be modest, Marshal. You saved my life as well as your own." Aurora's chin trembled a little, but that was the only outward sign of what she had to be feeling. She had nearly been killed and had lost her headquarters building, as well as the place where she had been living. Longarm admired her control.

He got to his feet, brushed off his clothes, then offered her a hand. The cook was already helping her up, however, and the men who had come boiling out of the sawmill after the crash were gathering around her as well, shouting anxious, excited questions.

The rattle of hoofbeats caught Longarm's attention, and he looked upstream to see Jared Flint galloping back toward them along the creek bank. "Miz McEntire!" he called before he even brought the horse to a halt. "Are you all right?"

Aurora nodded as Flint reined in, dismounted, and strode quickly toward her. The sawmill workers gathered around her parted to let the foreman through. "I'm fine, Mr. Flint," she told him, "just shaken up a little. Marshal Long's quick action saved my life."

Flint looked at Longarm and gave him a curt nod. "Much obliged, Marshal. We couldn't keep going around here without Miz McEntire."

"I want to know how this happened," Aurora said sharply. "That boom wasn't supposed to be floating loose like that."

The cook spoke up. "I seen it comin' lickety-split down the creek, Miz McEntire, and it looked like it was headin' either for your cabin or for the mill. That's why I come a-runnin' like that, tryin' to warn you."

Aurora smiled at him. "Thank you, Eli. You did all you

24

could." She glanced over at the ruined cabin and shook her head sadly. "I'm glad we escaped with our lives, but this is still quite a blow."

Flint walked around the rubble and moved out onto the boom, which looked like a mighty precarious perch to Longarm. The timberman was evidently used to stepping from log to log, though, and he quickly made his way to the back of the crude raft. Some of the ropes that had been used to bind the logs together had snapped under the impact of the crash, and the timber shifted with a series of groanings and scrapings. Aurora watched what Flint was doing, and anxiously caught her lower lip between her teeth as the foreman balanced himself carefully and reached down to haul a thick rope out of the water.

"Cut!" he yelled harshly as he turned toward the bank and waved the end of the rope. "Just like that pulley rope! Somebody sawed through it and let the boom get away early."

Longarm picked up his hat and slapped it against his leg to knock the dust off. As he settled the Stetson on his head, he said, "How could anybody cut that boom loose and know that it would wreck the headquarters building?"

"They couldn't," replied Aurora, "not for sure. But they could be pretty sure that it would do some damage to *something*, as fast as the creek is running. A small boom like that, released prematurely before more logs could be fastened to it, would be carried along so quickly that it was bound to get out of control."

Seemed like sort of a haphazard way to foul things up, Longarm thought with a frown, but he couldn't argue with the result. Even though chance had played a part in it, this latest act had had serious, almost lethal, consequences. As it had turned out, he and Aurora could have easily been killed.

Flint hopped agilely across the logs back to shore and came up to Longarm and Aurora. "I'll have some of the boys start going through the cabin," he said. "We'll salvage as much as we can, Miz McEntire."

"Thank you," said Aurora. "I think . . . I think I'll go over to the mess hall and sit down for a little while."

"Good idea," Longarm said. He turned to Flint and went

25

on, "I'd appreciate it if you'd send a man upstream to where that boom got loose, find out if anybody up there saw anything suspicious."

Flint nodded. "That's what I figured to do. What about you, Marshal?" His tone was faintly challenging.

"I was about to head for Kinsman's spread when that boom rammed the cabin. Reckon that's what I'll go ahead and do."

"Are you going to arrest him?" Again the challenge was in Flint's voice.

"Not without some proof," Longarm said flatly.

Flint glared at him for a second, then turned away to get the rest of the men busy on their tasks. Some of them headed back into the mill to keep it going, while the others began picking through the rubble of the cabin, trying to retrieve anything that could still be used.

Longarm walked with Aurora over to the mess hall. "Don't mind Mr. Flint," she said. "He's just worried."

Longarm wasn't sure if that was it or not. Flint had acted so upset and worried that Longarm had to wonder if the man possessed feelings for Aurora above and beyond those of a foreman for his boss. She'd been a widow for a couple of years, she had said. Maybe Flint had decided it was time to change that.

With that speculation in his mind, Longarm said his good-byes to Aurora and swung up onto the roan, which thankfully hadn't jerked its reins loose from the hitching rack and run off when the boom crashed into the cabin. He took the trail on which Flint had led him up to the camp earlier in the afternoon, and when he got to the guard shack, the man who had accosted him on his arrival stepped out of the shack and nodded to him. "Heading back to town, Marshal?" he asked.

"Not just yet," Longarm told the man, recalling that his name was Andy. "Can you tell me how to get to Matt Kinsman's ranch?" Andy frowned darkly at that question, and Longarm went on. "Your boss and Mr. Flint know I'm headed there. I'm trying to get to the bottom of the trouble around here."

"Then you're headed for the right place," said Andy. "Kinsman and his damned cowboys are to blame for everything that's gone wrong around here lately."

And Andy didn't even know about the latest incident, Longarm thought. If he did, he would have been ready to go to the Diamond K too. Only his goal would have been the exact opposite of Longarm's. Andy and the other loggers *wanted* a shooting war.

Unless he was able to come up with some answers pretty quick, Longarm told himself grimly, that was probably just what they were all going to get.

Matt Kinsman's spread wasn't hard to find. Longarm would have been able to locate it even without the directions furnished by Andy. Once he reached the main trail, he continued north for another half mile, then veered to the west on a narrower path.

Kinsman's range was fenced, and Longarm had to pass through a gate in the barbed wire. He latched it behind him and rode on, but he hadn't gone far when he heard a horse coming from the other direction.

He reined in and waited. There was a straight stretch of trail in front of him and whoever was coming, Longarm preferred to get a good look at them, rather than running head-on into them at a bend in the trail. The rider came into view a moment later, mounted on an Appaloosa. Longarm thought for a second it was a young man. Then he saw the long red hair falling free underneath the flat-crowned hat. He saw as well the way smallish breasts bobbed enticingly under a rather tight man's shirt.

That was Matt Kinsman's daughter riding toward him, Longarm realized, the young woman he had seen being met at the train station in Timber City by some of Kinsman's cowhands. The pace of the Appaloosa faltered a little as she noticed him sitting there waiting for her, but she came on steadily after that, startled perhaps by his unexpected presence but obviously unafraid to confront him.

He saw why she wasn't afraid of him when she drew rein some thirty feet away and slipped a Winchester carbine from a saddle sheath. With a smooth, crisp movement, she worked the carbine's lever action and pointed the barrel at him. "Who are you and what are you doing here?" she called.

27

"It's not very hospitable to point a gun at a fella when he hasn't given you any reason for doing it," Longarm pointed out, keeping his hands in plain sight as he rested them on the saddle horn.

"You're on Diamond K range," said the young woman, "and we've had more than our share of troubles lately. If you're a rustler or an outlaw, the only thing waiting for you around here is a slug."

Her voice was taut, angry. Longarm recalled the ticket agent in Timber City mentioning that Kinsman had had some problems of his own recently, such as rustlers and possibly poisoned wells. Must've been something to that, Longarm reflected, because the young woman was clearly on edge. At this moment, she would have just as soon shot him as looked at him.

Longarm didn't want that, of course—but he didn't want to reveal his true identity either. Aurora McEntire, Jared Flint, and some of the other members of the lumber crew knew that he was a lawman, but no one here on the Diamond K did. Might be best to keep it that way for a spell.

"I'm no outlaw," he said, "and I've never rustled a steer in my life. I'm just a chuck-line rider, looking for a riding job."

"Who told you to come out here?"

"Fella in town said the Diamond K was the best spread in these parts," Longarm replied honestly. "Thought I'd come out and talk to the boss, see if maybe there was a job to be had." He added dryly, "You ain't him, are you?"

The carbine's barrel lowered slightly. "You already know a man named Matt Kinsman owns this ranch. He's my father. I'm Molly Kinsman."

"Name's Custis," Longarm introduced himself.

She nodded and walked her horse a few steps closer. "Not a very common name."

"It's the one my mama gave me, back in West-by-God-Virginia."

"So you hail from West Virginia. I've never been there. But I spent the last two years in a school in Massachusetts."

Longarm grinned. "Should I offer you my condolences?"

28

Unexpectedly, she laughed, a bright, clear sound. "Might be appropriate," she said. "After growing up out here in the West, I like to have stifled back East. The teachers at Miss Hallowell's Academy for Young Ladies taught me a lot of things, but they don't know jack shit about ropin' or brandin'."

Longarm's grin widened into a laugh of his own. Now that she wasn't so suspicious of him, Molly Kinsman was turning into a downright likable young woman. He said, "You mind taking me on to the ranch headquarters?"

"Sure. You didn't think I was going to let you wander around our range by yourself, did you? Just because you say you're not a rustler doesn't mean it's necessarily true."

She had a point there, but at least she wasn't aiming that Winchester at him anymore. He heeled the roan into a walk that carried him alongside her as she sheathed the carbine and turned her own horse around.

"Are you just out for a ride, Miss Kinsman," he asked, "or were you looking for strays like me?"

"I like to ride," she said, not really answering his question but coming close enough. "And I pick up strays wherever I find them."

Longarm chuckled. Young Molly had a bold glint in her eye as she looked at him, he thought. Under other circumstances, he might've been tempted to find out just how bold she could be, but right now, he had a job to do.

Still, that didn't stop him from appreciating the way that red hair blew out behind her as she rode, or the intriguing movements of her breasts under her shirt, or the fine curve of her slender hips in a pair of denim trousers. He was willing to bet she was a ring-tailed terror when her Irish was up, but if a man was strong enough to hang on and keep up with her, it would be a hell of a ride.

They had cantered a mile or so up the trail when more riders appeared, trotting on horseback toward them. Molly slowed her horse and muttered something under her breath, but Longarm couldn't make it out. She turned to him and said, "Let me handle this."

"Yes, ma'am," Longarm said mildly. "This is your

daddy's ranch, after all, and I expect those are some of his riders.''

"They are.''

Molly brought her horse to a halt, and Longarm followed suit. The cowboys riding toward them actually picked up the pace at the sight of them, so that their horses kicked up a little dust when they brought them to skidding stops about ten feet from Longarm and Molly.

The man in the lead, who looked to be in his early twenties, thumbed back his hat on a thatch of shaggy blond hair and demanded, "Molly, what the hell are you doin' ridin' around out here by yourself? And who's this long drink of water?''

"I can ride wherever I want, whenever I want, Seth Thomas,'' responded Molly, her voice sharp with annoyance. "And this gentleman is named Custis. He's come here looking for work.''

The young cowboy called Seth snorted. "Ain't no work around here for saddle tramps. You might as well turn around and go back where you came from, mister.''

"You stay right there, Custis,'' snapped Molly. To Seth she said, "It's not up to you who gets hired around here. That's a decision my father and Joe Traywick make. Last time I looked, Joe was still the foreman of the Diamond K, not you.''

Seth glared at her, and Longarm got the idea that he wasn't particularly happy that someone else was the ranch foreman. Could be Seth had his eye on that job for himself.

He sure had his eye on Molly, Longarm added to himself. Though Seth had been barely civil to her so far, he had that certain look about him. Longarm had seen it before. Given half a chance, Seth would be so moon-eyed over Molly that he could scarcely stand up.

Which was neither here nor there where his assignment was concerned, Longarm reminded himself. He swung his gaze to the other four riders and saw that they were all youngsters too, likely Seth's pards who would follow his lead.

"I'm not looking for any trouble,'' said Longarm. "I'll just talk to Mr. Kinsman, and if he doesn't have any work for me, I'll move on.''

"Damn right you will,'' Seth said unpleasantly. "And if

30

you don't, I'll kick your ass right off this ranch, old man."

Longarm sighed. Some folks you just couldn't be polite to. He leaned forward in the saddle and said, "Why don't you get down off that horse?"

Seth's eyes lit up with excitement as he replied, "You just bet I will!" He began to hurriedly dismount.

"Custis, don't," Molly said, reaching over to put a hand on his arm. "Seth's just young and hotheaded. He didn't mean any harm."

"You hush up, woman!" called Seth. "This ain't any of your business anymore."

Longarm smiled faintly. "Don't worry, Miss Kinsman. I reckon I'm so old and stove-up it won't take long for Seth here to take care of me. Maybe he won't hurt me too bad."

Seth already had his gunbelt off. He coiled it around his saddlehorn and then hung his hat on top of it. When he turned back toward Longarm, he brought his clenched fists up in a crude imitation of a professional boxer.

"Where'd you learn that stance, from pictures in the *Police Gazette*?" Longarm asked as he stepped down from the roan and took off his own gunbelt and hat. He handed them to Molly to hold, then started to turn back toward Seth.

With a yell that was echoed by shouts of encouragement from his friends, Seth charged forward, swinging wildly. Longarm tipped his head back a little and let the first punch whip harmlessly in front of him. Then he leaned to the side as Seth's momentum carried him past. Longarm stuck the toe of his boot between Seth's ankles and sent the young cowboy sprawling to the ground.

Seth landed hard, the breath coming out of him with an *oof!* Longarm stepped back and watched as Seth rolled over and came up furious and gasping for air. "You son of a bitch! That wasn't fair!"

"You got a few years on me, as you so kindly pointed out," said Longarm. "Figured it was all right for me to even the odds a mite."

"I'm goin' to kill you!" Once again, the cowboy charged. This time Longarm blocked the first punch and then straightened Seth up with a short, hard right to the face. Seth's head rocked back from the blow. Before he could recover, Longarm stepped closer and hooked a left into his belly. Seth lost his breath again. Worse, he doubled over so that his jaw was in perfect position for the looping right Longarm brought around. He fell like a sack of potatoes dropped from the back of a wagon.

Longarm stepped back, not even breathing hard. "Just so you know," he said to the feebly writhing figure on the ground, "it ain't the years that put age on a man, old son. It's the miles."

The other young cowhands were looking on in amazement, clearly stunned that Longarm had disposed of Seth so easily. Longarm glanced at them to make sure that none of them were showing any signs of taking up the gauntlet for their fallen friend, then turned back toward Molly. He heard Seth stagger to his feet behind him.

"You . . . you . . ." Seth gasped. Longarm didn't stop or look around. "You bastard!" Seth finally got out. "I'll . . . kill you!"

Longarm glanced back and saw Seth lunging toward his horse. The cowboy reached his mount and clawed at the holstered revolver looped over the saddlehorn. As the gun came free and Seth started to turn, Molly drew her carbine and brought it up. "No, Seth!" she cried. "I'll drop you in your tracks if you cock that gun!"

"Molly!" Seth practically wailed. "You . . . you wouldn't!"

"Damn right I would." A faint quaver in Molly's voice revealed the strain she was under.

"Good Lord," Longarm muttered. "The antics of you youngsters are a vexation, pure and simple. I didn't knock *all* the brains out of your head, Seth. Use what you've got left and put that gun away before the lady has to shoot you. I imagine it'd plumb ruin her day to have to kill you."

For a second, Longarm thought one of them was going to be foolish enough to start shooting anyway. Then, with a disgusted curse, Seth shoved his pistol back in its holster. "Reckon it ain't worth dyin' over," he said. He pointed a finger at Longarm. "But one of these days, you and me are goin' to finish this!"

Anything Longarm could have said would just make the situation worse, he decided, so he didn't say anything at all. He picked up his hat and gunbelt, which Molly had dropped to draw the Winchester, and made sure the .44 was all right before he strapped the belt around his waist. For the second time today, he knocked dust off his hat—it was starting to look more gray than brown, he reflected—and put it on. "I reckon if you're ready, Miss Kinsman, we'll ride on to the ranch and see your father."

"Won't be necessary," said one of the other cowboys, speaking up for the first time. "Here comes Big Matt now!"

Chapter 4

Longarm turned and saw another group of riders coming toward them, led by a tall, broad-shouldered man on a deep-chested black stallion. He wore a sheepskin coat that flapped open over a woolen shirt. The outfit was probably a little warm for this time of year, thought Longarm, but it didn't seem to bother the man. His hair under the broad-brimmed hat he wore was a mixture of gray and bright red, so now Longarm knew where Molly got her flaming tresses.

And her temper. As the riders came up, the big redheaded man barked, "What in the name o' the seven imps o' Satan is goin' on here? You been fightin' again, Seth? Damn it, boy, I warned you that if you didn't stop thinkin' with your fists, I'd boot your butt from here to Kansas, and by God, I've got half a mind to do just that!"

The rider beside him, a middle-aged man with a seamed face and a thick, graying mustache, said quietly, "Better take it easy, Matt. You know the doc over in Portland said it'd be better for you if you stopped gettin' so riled up all the time."

"To hell with that sawbones and all the other pill-pushers!"

Matt Kinsman exploded. "Where in blazes were all of them when I was carvin' a ranch out of the wilderness? Answer me that, Joe!"

Joe Traywick just shook his head. He looked over at Seth and said, "Get your hat and gun on, boy, and get mounted up. I want up all of you up in that northwest pasture, pronto."

Muttering a little—but casting leery glances toward Kinsman as he did so—Seth did as he was instructed. A moment later, he and his friends were galloping off.

Besides Kinsman and Traywick, there were two more riders with them. Like Traywick, they were older hands who were probably some of Kinsman's longtime, trusted riders. Kinsman watched Seth and the younger men leave, then turned his attention to Longarm and asked, "Who the hell're you?"

Despite the brusque attitude, Longarm sensed that Kinsman wasn't really as unfriendly as he sounded. The rancher had undoubtedly endured a great many hardships while he was establishing the Diamond K, and it was in his nature now to be curt. That was different from Seth's behavior. The young cowboy had been *trying* to be a horse's ass.

Longarm nodded respectfully and said to the rancher, "Howdy, Mr. Kinsman. My name's Custis, and I'm looking for work."

"Sort of long in the tooth to be a cowboy, aren't you?"

"I've been to see the elephant a time or two," admitted Longarm. "That don't mean I can't dab a loop on a proddy steer or chouse mavericks out of the brush."

"Mavericks, eh? Texan?"

"Been there a heap of times. Ain't from there."

Kinsman didn't ask where Longarm *was* from. He just said, "What do you think, Joe?"

Traywick regarded Longarm intently for a moment, then said, "We could use another man or two, Matt. We're spread kind of thin, and with all the trouble that's been goin' on . . ."

Kinsman looked sharply at Longarm. "You heard my foreman. There's been some trouble in this part of the country, Custis. You sure you want to mix in? No offense taken if you decide to ride on."

35

"I've been around trouble too," Longarm said. "It never bothered me overmuch."

"Good enough," Kinsman said with an abrupt nod. "You're hired." He gave a booming laugh, demonstrating that his moods could change like quicksilver. "If nothin' else, havin' you around'll be a burr under Seth's saddle, after the way you whipped him. Dose of humility'll do that boy some good, I hope." He looked over at Molly and frowned. "What're you doin' out here, girl? Thought you was back at the house."

"I wanted to take a ride," explained Molly. "I happened to run into Custis down close to the main trail."

"Just happened to run into him, huh. Was he a gentleman?"

"A perfect gentleman," Molly said with a quick smile for Longarm.

"Good, I won't have to shoot him then." Kinsman wheeled his horse and jerked his head to indicate that the others should follow him. "Come on, Custis. Too late in the afternoon to get you started today. You can have supper with us and get settled into the bunkhouse."

"Sure," Longarm agreed easily. "My warbag and Winchester are back in Timber City, but I reckon I can pick 'em up in a day or two, soon as I get a spare minute."

"Cook'll be goin' into town day after tomorrow to pick up supplies," said Joe Traywick. "You can go with him and help load the wagon. That'll give you a chance to get your gear."

"Sounds good," said Longarm. He instinctively liked Traywick. He wasn't so sure about Kinsman just yet.

Of course, he didn't want to get too fond of anybody on the Diamond K.

Not when he might have to arrest some of them for murder.

The headquarters of the Diamond K lay in a beautiful lower valley with the peaks of the Cascade range towering above it. The grass in the pastures was thick and lush, the green landscape dotted with grazing jags of cattle. The ranch house itself stood among a group of pines. It was an impressive structure, three stories of stone and whitewashed timber. Longarm took in the other features of the ranch: a high-ceilinged hay barn,

36

a chicken house, extensive corrals and a barn for the spread's horses, a blacksmith shop, a cookshack, and a bunkhouse. A fence built of peeled pine poles enclosed a well-cared-for yard in front of the house.

Big Matt Kinsman brought his black stallion to a halt on a small rise that overlooked the ranch headquarters, and the riders with him did likewise. For Longarm's benefit, Kinsman waved a hand at the buildings and said, "This is the Diamond K, Custis. Built the house with my own two hands for my late wife, Molly's mother. She's been gone five years now."

"Sorry to hear it," Longarm said, and meant the words.

Kinsman nodded. "Alice was a hell of a woman, let me tell you. Would've liked to have more kids, but Molly was the only one that ever came along." He glanced over at his daughter. "Not that we were ever disappointed in her, mind you. She's the best child a man could want."

"It's just too bad you can't seem to remember that whenever you're laying down the law to me, Pa," she said.

Kinsman scowled. "Every child needs firm instruction in what's right and what's wrong—and it's wrong for a gal to sass her daddy like that."

"Yes, well, you can't punish me if you can't catch me," said Molly with a roguish grin. "And we all know I can ride rings around you any day."

As if to prove it, she heeled her horse into a run. It leaped ahead, carrying her toward the ranch house. Her hair streamed out behind her as she leaned forward over the neck of the racing horse, and Longarm thought that made an even prettier picture than the scenery on display.

Kinsman chuckled. "She's a mite headstrong, but one of these days the right man will come along and love all the devil out of her."

"We can hope so anyway," Joe Traywick said dryly, " 'fore she's the death of you an' me both, Matt!"

Kinsman put his horse into a walk. Longarm, Traywick, and the other two riders followed him. When they reached the ranch headquarters, Kinsman headed for the big house, saying over his shoulder, "Show Custis the ropes, Joe."

"Sure will, Matt," Traywick agreed.

The other two riders trotted over to the horse barn. Traywick swung down from his saddle and motioned for Longarm to do the same. They led their mounts toward the barn, and as they walked, Traywick pointed out most of the things Longarm had already noticed about the place. Now that he got a closer look at everything, Longarm was struck by how it was all in top shape and good repair. If the Diamond K was truly having trouble, a fella couldn't tell it by looking at the place.

"Tell me the truth, Custis," Traywick said after a brief moment of silence. "How long has it been since you did any real cowboying?"

Longarm pondered, then admitted, "It's been a while. I reckon you don't ever forget how to work with cows, though, after you've learned it."

"Probably not," Traywick grunted. "But what I'm interested in is what you've been doin' in the meantime." He gestured at the .44 in Longarm's cross-draw rig. "You sell your skills with that?"

Longarm drew himself up indignantly. "I'm no hired gun, if that's what you mean. I can use a hogleg, but I've never shot anybody who didn't have it coming."

"What about gambling? You a tinhorn?"

This time Longarm grinned at the question. "I'll own up to enjoying a friendly game of poker, and I've bucked the tiger at faro a time or two. But I've never made a living with the pasteboards, nor had a hankering to."

Traywick nodded. "Don't mean no offense by askin' so many questions, Custis. It's just that I've been with Matt Kinsman for a long time, and I sort of look out after him. I reckon you understand."

"Sure do," Longarm assured the foreman. "I'll be honest with you, Mr. Traywick, I'm the fiddle-footed sort. Spend most of my time drifting from place to place, just seeing what's on the other side of the hill. But whenever I light in a place, I give my boss an honest day's work for as long as I'm there. You got my word on that."

"I'll take it," Traywick said as he extended his hand. "Welcome to the Diamond K, Custis. You'll be treated fair here."

Longarm shook the man's hand, feeling the calluses that years of working with a rope had put there. Now that he had been accepted by the foreman, Longarm thought he might risk a question or two of his own.

"What's this about problems you've been having in these parts? Seems plumb peaceful to me."

Traywick sighed and shook his head. "That's because you just ain't been around here long enough. I swear, I'm afraid somebody's goin' to get killed 'fore it's all over." Venom came into the man's voice, sounding odd because Longarm was already accustomed to Traywick's normally mild tone. "And it's all the fault of those damned lumberjacks!"

"There's a logging outfit around here?" Longarm asked innocently.

"Three or four of 'em in this part of the Cascades alone." Traywick jerked a thumb toward the timbered slopes of the mountain rising above the ranch. "It's the bunch operatin' right up yonder that's causin' all the trouble, though. I'd stake my liver on it."

"Bad blood between them and the Diamond K, huh?"

"It all started when we lost some cows to rustlers a while back," said Traywick. "Matt and I rode up there to that lumber camp to find out if maybe they'd seen or heard anybody movin' cattle durin' the night, and damned if they wasn't all sittin' around eatin' steaks!"

"You think lumberjacks rustled your beef?" That sounded pretty unlikely to Longarm. Those timbermen might know their way around a knife and a fork, but most of them weren't any good with steaks still on the hoof.

"I'm convinced of it. That woman who's runnin' the place claimed they hadn't seen any sign of anything suspicious."

"What about the steaks?"

"Said they bought 'em in Timber City."

"Well, I reckon that's possible," said Longarm.

"Sure, but it's just as likely they stole those cows from us," Traywick said stubbornly. "Matt practically said as much, and that woman got her dander up and told us to get out. Matt told her that bein' a gentleman, he wouldn't call her a liar to her face—but it was plain that was what he thought of her."

That agreed with what Aurora McEntire had said . . . almost. She had left out any mention of steaks cooking and rustled beeves. Longarm said, "I've heard tell that some of those logging outfits cut down so much timber that the runoff from the rains does a lot of damage to the range down below. That true in this case?"

"Well, not so much." The admission on the foreman's part was grudging. "I reckon it's just a matter of time, though. Sooner or later, so many of the trees'll be gone that none of the soil will hold. That'll cause flooding down here, and erosion will foul the streams too." Traywick shook his head. "No, sir, ranching and logging just don't go together."

"Those loggers pulled any other tricks?"

"Less'n a week after Matt and me rode up there, one of our wells in a dry pasture went bad. Couple of dozen head died from drinking at the stock tank we filled from it. If you ask me, those lumberjacks poured poison down it."

"But you can't prove that."

Traywick looked at Longarm with slitted eyes. "Say, what're you actin' so doubtful about? You intend to ride for the brand or not?"

"Sure, I do," Longarm said quickly. "I just like to know who's on the other side if I'm getting into a fight."

"Well, now you know." Traywick jerked his head toward the barn. "Let's get these nags unsaddled and rubbed down. I'm tired of flappin' my jaw."

What he had said so far was interesting enough, thought Longarm. Matt Kinsman was hotheaded and held a grudge, and it was possible the friction between the Diamond K and the McEntire Timber Company had started over a few rustled cows that the loggers hadn't really had anything to do with. Was Kinsman the sort to strike back at the timber operation and get some men killed just to satisfy a grudge? Longarm couldn't answer that question for certain, but his instincts said no. However, he didn't know all the men who rode for the Diamond K, and for that matter, he had already met one who flew off the handle and resorted to violence mighty quick.

Seth Thomas.

As Longarm unsaddled the roan, rubbed it down, and settled

it in a stall with grain and water, he reflected on what he had learned so far. The loggers and the cowboys hated each other; whether for good reason or not didn't matter. He could easily imagine Seth and some of his cronies trying to strike back at the lumberjacks for imagined injustices, which would in turn lead the timbermen to try to get even by poisoning wells and such. It was a cycle of violence that could escalate into a bloody, full-scale war unless somebody tamped out the flames mighty soon. That somebody, of course, was him.

And his theory, if it was correct, still left unanswered the question of who had rustled Kinsman's stock in the first place.

Longarm was going to have to ponder on that later. As he and Traywick left the barn, the sound of the dinner bell being rung came from the ranch house. The sun had already slipped behind the peaks of the Cascades to the west.

Traywick led Longarm to the house. As they walked toward it, several other men appeared from various places around the headquarters, all converging on the big house in response to the clangorous summons of the cook ringing the bell. He was a wizened little Chinaman, Longarm noted, who had probably come to this country during the construction of the Central Pacific Railroad a little more than a decade earlier. A lot of those former coolies had a way with grub, Longarm knew, so he expected dinner would be good.

The inside of the house showed the same care as the outside. Molly had been away at school in the East for several years, so it wasn't a particularly feminine place, but Longarm could see a woman's hand at work here and there. The windows all had curtains on them, and the rugs were clean. Chairs and sofas made of heavy wood and thickly cushioned were scattered around the big main room. Through a wide doorway with a thick beam above it was the dining room, complete with a long table that had been polished to a high shine. A glass-fronted cabinet on one side of the room contained the late Mrs. Kinsman's china and crystal, and all of it sparkled in the light of the oil-burning chandelier that hung over the table. The place settings tonight weren't anything fancy, but the plates and cups and silverware were functional enough to suit the cowboys who were gathering around the table.

The table itself was loaded with platters of food. Longarm saw steaks and fried chicken, bowls full of mashed potatoes and green beans, corn on the cob, steamed carrots, biscuits, gravy, and sliced tomatoes. Longarm felt hunger pangs clutch at his belly. The lunch he had grabbed quickly in Timber City before riding out had been both meager and a long time ago. He was ready to eat.

Matt Kinsman was already seated at the head of the table, with Molly at his right hand. Joe Traywick took the chair at the other end of the table. There was a vacant seat to his left, and he gestured for Longarm to take it. As Longarm did so, he looked across the table and found himself staring into the angry face of the young cowboy, Seth Thomas. Seth's jaw was already starting to turn purple where Longarm had clouted him.

There weren't any other empty chairs, and to move at this point wouldn't have looked very good anyway, so there was nothing left to do except brazen it out. Longarm smiled and nodded at Seth, who just glowered that much more. A glance at the other end of the table told Longarm that Molly was watching what was going on, but he couldn't read the expression on her face.

"Say grace for us, Joe," rumbled Kinsman, and all the cowboys bowed their heads. Traywick muttered a blessing. Then, almost as one, eager hands shot out toward the platters of food, and the next few minutes were filled with the clatter of silverware as the cowboys served themselves and passed along the platters.

Longarm heaped his plate and dug in with enthusiasm. The Chinese cook carried around a coffeepot and filled everyone's cup. There was glasses of buttermilk too, cool enough so that little beads of moisture formed on the outside. The meal was every bit as good as Longarm expected it to be.

Like most of the other ranch crews he had been around, these men weren't talkative when there was serious business like eating to be taken care of. Conversation would come later in the bunkhouse, while they were playing cards or mending tack or whittling or just shooting the breeze. Though he would never go back to it, cowboying wasn't a bad way to live,

Longarm thought. The work was hard and sometimes dangerous, the pay was poor at best, but it was a life that had its
own special rewards.

Sort of like being a deputy United States marshal.

When the meal was over, most of the hands headed for the
bunkhouse. Seth gave Longarm an especially baleful stare before he went. Longarm returned the look blandly, not letting
the youngster see that he was getting a little annoyed. As Matt
Kinsman scraped back his chair and stood up, he said, "Joe,
you and Custis stay here a minute, if you don't mind."

"Sure, Matt," said Traywick, and Longarm nodded.

Kinsman turned to his daughter. "Molly, you can go on
upstairs."

"What if I don't want to?" she asked. She had changed
into a simple dress with little blue and yellow flowers all over
it, and Longarm thought she looked mighty pretty.

"Blast it, girl, I'm goin' to be talkin' business," Kinsman
said with a scowl.

"And who's going to be running this ranch someday?" said
Molly.

"Your husband, damn it!"

Molly made a delicate sound of utter disdain that Longarm
imagined must have been part of the curriculum back there in
Massachusetts at Miss Hallowell's Academy for Young Ladies. Every woman he had ever encountered had known how
to make it, from soiled doves to countesses, so he figured
somebody had to be teaching it somewhere.

Kinsman was just as stubborn as his daughter, however, and
after a few minutes of stubborn, mutually glowering silence,
Molly gave up and left the dining room. Longarm heard her
steps on the stairs leading up to the second and third floors.
He wondered idly which floor her bedroom was on . . . not that
he was likely to be finding out.

Kinsman led Longarm and Traywick into his study, the
walls of which were lined with bookshelves and gun racks. As
he sat down behind a big desk, the rancher asked Longarm,
"Did Joe fill you in on the trouble we've been havin' around
here?"

Longarm nodded. "Yes, sir, he did."

"You look like a man who's seen a mite of trouble in his time," said Kinsman bluntly. "That's one of the reasons I hired you. What do you think of the situation?"

Carefully, Longarm said, "Sounds like those lumberjacks up on the mountain are a mite too big for their britches."

"Damn right," said Kinsman with a snort. "They're behind all of it, I'll warrant. And I'll not take any more from them, either. Next timber-cutter I find gettin' up to mischief on my range, he's goin' to rue the day he was born, by God!"

"Maybe you ought to take the fight to them," suggested Longarm casually. It wasn't likely Kinsman would admit to a near stranger that he was behind the problems up at the lumber camp, but anything was possible. Sometimes long shots paid off.

But not this time. Kinsman scowled and shook his head vehemently. "Nope. I ain't one to hunt trouble, and as long as I'm left alone, I'll leave the other fella to go on about his business." His fist came down on the desk with a thump. "But I'll not be trifled with neither. I just want you to know, Custis—you find any of those lumberjacks on Diamond K range, you handle it however you see fit and I'll back you up on it. I wouldn't say that to all of my hands—some of 'em are too young and hotheaded—but I figure you've been around enough to know what to do."

Longarm nodded solemnly. "As long as I'm drawing pay from you, I'll look out for your interests, Mr. Kinsman. You got my word on that." That wasn't exactly a lie, Longarm added to himself. He didn't intend to ever draw any wages from the rancher. He planned to have this case wrapped up and be long gone from Oregon by the time a month had rolled by.

Reaching for a drawer in the desk, Kinsman said, "Speakin' of pay, you need an advance? Again, I wouldn't say that to just anybody."

Longarm shook his head. "No, thanks. I didn't ride in here stone-cold broke, and I don't like to take money until I've earned it."

"Well, then, I reckon we're done." Kinsman stood up and extended his hand across the desk. "Welcome to the Diamond K,

Custis," he said, echoing what Traywick had said earlier.

Longarm shook hands with the rancher, then bade him good night. Traywick stayed behind to go over the books with Kinsman, and Longarm left the house to stroll toward the bunkhouse.

He detoured along the way and walked over to the horse barn instead, intending to check on the roan. He found a lantern on a hook just inside the door, lit it with a lucifer that he flicked into life on an iron-hard thumbnail, then walked along the broad central aisle to the stall where the roan was stabled. The horse whickered gently as Longarm reached over the gate to scratch its nose. There was still plenty of grain and water in the stall, so Longarm turned toward the front of the barn again, satisfied with this errand.

A figure stood there in the open doorway.

"What are you doing roaming around out here, Custis?" asked Molly Kinsman.

The sight of her had brought him up short. She moved quiet on her feet, like an Indian. That was something they *didn't* teach at Miss Hallowell's Academy. More than likely it was just natural grace on Molly's part. Longarm stood there by the stall and watched appreciatively as she walked toward him.

"Reckon I could ask you the same thing," he said. "I thought your daddy sent you upstairs."

"My daddy sends me a lot of places. I don't always go." She stopped in front of him, only about two feet separating them. "He thinks I'm going to settle down and get married— to some dull cowboy of his choice, naturally—and then do nothing but pop out one baby after another while my husband takes care of the important things, like running the ranch."

"You don't care much for that plan, do you?" Longarm said quietly.

"I know as much about running this ranch as anybody! At least, I would if he'd ever give me a chance. And I certainly don't intend to marry some ignorant puncher like Seth Thomas just to give my father some grandchildren."

"Nothing wrong with marrying a cowboy, I guess," Longarm said with a shrug of his shoulders.

"It's not what I want," insisted Molly. "I want a man

45

who's been places and done things. Maybe . . . somebody like you, Custis.''

She closed the distance between them, sliding her arms around his waist and pressing her body to his. Longarm reacted instinctively, his shaft hardening against the soft pressure of her belly. He hung the lantern on a hook so she wouldn't get up against it and burn herself. She was already hot enough.

But he was in no mood to get himself shot or strung up for taking advantage of an innocent young girl, so he backed off and said, "I ain't sure this is such a good idea."

"Don't worry about my virtue, Custis," she said in a husky voice as she moved with him. "I lost that less than a month after I arrived in Boston. But it's been a long time since I've been with a man like you." Her hand strayed down to the bulge at the crotch of his denims, tracing the length and heft of him through the material. She caught her breath. "Lord! Come to think of it, I don't believe I've ever been with a man exactly like you."

She kissed him then, her mouth hungrily seeking out his. Longarm's arms went around her of their own volition, pulling her more tightly against him. He could feel the erect buds of her nipples poking through the soft material of her dress. She moaned deep in her throat as she thrust her hips against his groin. Her mouth opened and her tongue flickered boldly around his.

The lantern was still burning and the doors of the barn were wide open, which meant that anybody who happened to walk by could look in and see them wrapped up in each other's arms. As tempting as the thought of taking Molly into one of the empty stalls for a roll in the hay—literally!—might be, he didn't want to ruin this investigation before it even got properly under way.

He put his hands on her shoulders and firmly moved her away from him. "This ain't a good idea, Molly," he said. "I don't reckon you're even half my age."

"I'm nineteen," she said.

"Close enough."

"And I already told you, I'm no blushing virgin. I know what I want, Custis."

46

Longarm took a deep breath. "That don't matter. I work for your daddy, and from what I've seen of him so far, he'd likely ventilate me if he caught me messing with his little girl. If he didn't, I reckon Joe probably would."

"You're afraid of my father?" Molly shook her head. "I don't think you're really afraid of anything, Custis." Again she cupped his groin brazenly. "Unless it's that you can't keep up with me."

"Lord," muttered Longarm under his breath. She was persistent, he had to give her that.

He wasn't sure what he should do, but fortunately, he didn't have to make the decision after all. Footsteps sounded outside the barn, and Molly suddenly gasped and stepped back away from him. She turned and walked swiftly toward the entrance, leaving Longarm behind her, blinking a little in surprise. Molly was mighty bold, all right . . . until she thought she was about to be caught.

As she left the barn, she passed Seth Thomas, who paused and lifted a hand toward her. "Molly?" he said. But she didn't stop, just continued toward the house.

Seth looked into the barn and saw Longarm standing there next to the stalls. "You!" he exclaimed. "What'd you do to Molly?"

"Not a thing," Longarm said. "Just checking on my horse before I turned in for the night." He reached out and took the lantern from the hook, then carried it up the aisle toward the entrance. When he reached the doors, he blew out the flame and replaced the lantern where he had found it.

"Wait just a damn minute!" Seth put a hand on Longarm's shoulder to stop him when Longarm started past. "You didn't tell me what Miss Kinsman was doing out here."

"If it's any of your business, she was doing the same thing I was—checking on her horse. Now I'll thank you to let me by." Longarm was tired, and he didn't bother trying to keep the annoyance out of his voice now.

Seth moved his hand and stepped back, but he managed to display some bravado as he said, "You better not cross me, mister. I may have to work with you, but I don't have to like you."

"Feeling's mutual," said Longarm. He took a cheroot from his vest pocket, put it in his mouth, and strode off before Seth could say anything else. As he walked, he scratched another lucifer into life and lit the cheroot, drawing deeply on it.

Had Molly known that Seth was headed toward the barn when she made her play for him? Longarm wondered. Could be she was just using him to make Seth jealous, despite all the things she had said about not liking the young cowboy. And even though Seth seemed to consider her some sort of pest, Longarm had already guessed the boy was more than half in love with her. This was just the sort of game a couple of feisty kids who were really attracted to each other might play.

He just shook his head, feeling old, and walked on toward the bunkhouse.

Chapter 5

Longarm hadn't forgotten how early cowboys got up. Joe Traywick rousted the hands out of their bunks the next morning when the sky was barely turning gray in the east. Longarm rose with the rest of them, trying not to groan. After this, he vowed, he would never again complain about Billy Vail wanting him to show up at the Federal Building in Denver by nine o'clock in the morning. He knew, of course, that he would break that vow about the second morning back from this assignment.

Molly didn't put in an appearance at breakfast, which came as no surprise. Longarm hadn't expected to see her at the table. Seth Thomas was there, though, still glaring at him. Longarm ignored the young man and listened as Traywick handed out the day's chores.

"Custis, you'll be with me today," concluded the foreman. "I'll see that you get the lay of the land."

Longarm nodded. "Fine by me."

The Arbuckle's was black and strong, and the Chinese cook piled up the flapjacks and bacon and scrambled eggs on each man's plate. Longarm ate heartily, and when he was finished, he felt considerably more alert and ready for the day that was stretching out in front of him. He went out to the barn with the other hands to saddle his horse, enjoying the cool morning air as he walked from the ranch house.

He had told Aurora McEntire and Jared Flint that he would try to get back to the lumber camp today to let them know what, if anything, he had found out. That might not be possible after all, since it was likely he would be riding with Joe Traywick all day. But Longarm was working his way in here at the Diamond K so well that he didn't want to risk ruining things. Aurora and Flint would just have to wait.

The night before, Longarm had listened carefully to the talk going on around him in the bunkhouse. He had thought that one of the cowboys might let something slip about making trouble for the McEntire lumber operation, but that hadn't proven to be the case. The conversation had been the usual mixture of jokes and boasts and jeers common to any gathering of cowhands. Clearly, if someone on the Diamond K was responsible for the timber company's problems, it was going to take longer to root him out.

Longarm didn't mind having the opportunity to tour the ranch with Traywick. Any time he was working, he liked to familiarize himself with the terrain. He had been to the western slopes of the Cascade range before, but not for a while and not this particular stretch of country.

Traywick proved to be a good companion too, an easy talker but not so long-winded about anything that he tired out a fella's ears. Longarm was the most interested when the foreman pointed out the boundaries of Diamond K range.

"That's all government land up there," said Traywick, waving a hand toward the upper slopes as he and Longarm reined in high on the shoulder of the mountain. "That McEntire woman has got a timber lease on it." His voice sounded like he had a bad taste in his mouth.

Longarm crossed his hands on the saddlehorn and leaned forward to ease his muscles. "How far north does their lease run?" he asked casually.

Traywick snorted. "Damned if I know—or care. It runs out

somewhere, though, because there's another outfit loggin' those slopes over yonder. Belongs to a fella named Callahan.''

Longarm filed that nugget of information away. He doubted that it would ever prove useful, but he wanted to remain in the habit of taking note of things.

He and Traywick continued their loop, which would eventually take them back to the ranch headquarters. The Chinese cook had packed lunches for them—fried chicken legs left over from the night before, biscuits, and a little jar of marmalade that made Longarm lick his lips in delight when they stopped to eat at midday. They arrived back at headquarters late in the afternoon. Most of the other hands were still out on the range, including Seth Thomas, so Longarm didn't have to contend with the proddy kid for a change.

Molly was standing at one of the corral fences, however, a booted foot propped on the bottom rail as she watched a couple of cowboys trying to gentle some half-wild horses. She was wearing jeans and a man's shirt again, and Longarm admired the way the clothes showed off her breasts and backside. She glanced over her shoulder and caught him looking at her, and he felt unaccountably foolish. She had a way of keeping him off balance, and that was unusual.

He led his horse into the barn, following Traywick, and commented, "The boss's daughter seems like a pretty high-spirited filly."

"That she is," agreed Traywick. "She didn't much want Matt sendin' her off to school like that after her mama passed on, but he wouldn't be talked out of it. Said that with Alice gone, the ranch was no place for a young girl. I expect he was right . . . but it was still hard on Molly." The foreman shot a warning glance at Longarm. "I wouldn't take it kindly if anybody was to ever hurt that gal."

"Figured that much already," said Longarm. "I wouldn't want to do her any harm, Joe. You got my word on that."

Traywick nodded. "Good. Glad to hear it."

Of course, Longarm reflected, having heard Molly's boasts about her lusty exploits back in Boston, it was debatable whether or not he would be harming her by a friendly little romp. That seemed to be exactly what she wanted.

51

But it would sure as blazes complicate his current chore, which was to get proof of who was attacking Aurora McEntire's timber operation and put a stop to it. Business before pleasure, Longarm reminded himself.

That was a good rule . . . but one that wasn't always easy to follow.

The next morning after breakfast, Longarm and the Chinese cook, whose name was Wing, got on the spring wagon that had been used to pick up Molly at the train station and headed for Timber City. Wing had a long list of supplies he needed for the ranch's kitchen, and Longarm was supposed to help him load them onto the wagon, along with several rolls of barbed wire. On the way into town, Wing chattered incessantly in a sort of pidgin English. Longarm smoked and didn't pay much attention to what the Chinaman was saying.

Suddenly one of Wing's comments intruded itself on his attention. "Missy Molly ver' pretty, ver' smart. Make some man good wife, you bet."

Longarm grinned over at his companion. "You trying to marry me off to your boss's daughter, Wing?"

"Just telling you. Missy Molly like Custis. Wing see it in eyes."

"Well, old son, you'd better just keep on looking, because I ain't the sort to settle down. Though I'll agree that Miss Molly is mighty pretty and mighty smart."

"Diamond K good spread. Man who marry Missy Molly wind up with ranch too."

Longarm threw back his head and laughed. "You're a hell of a salesman, Wing. But like I said, I ain't the kind of man she needs."

The cook shrugged and said, "Cannot blame Wing for trying."

"No, I reckon not." Longarm played a hunch and went on. "What do you think about all the troubles Mr. Kinsman's been having lately? You reckon those loggers are behind it, like him and Mr. Traywick think they are?"

"Wing cook once for logging camp. Timber men hate cowboys. Not like 'em at all. Ver' much hard feelings." Wing's

52

head bobbed up and down. "Lumberjacks could try hurt Diamond K."

"You've been around timber cutters before, you said. Did you ever run across any of 'em who knew one end of a cow from the other?"

Wing frowned. "Lumberjacks not like cattle, except eat."

"That's right. Seems to me like they'd have had a hard time rustling very many steers, especially since whoever did that was so slick they didn't even leave a trail."

"Wing not think of that. Confused now."

"You and me both, old son," Longarm told him. "You and me both."

The previous night Longarm had again listened closely in the bunkhouse for anything that might give away the culprits, and again he had come up empty. This was turning into an odd case. There was trouble on both sides of the argument, and he had likely suspects for all the wrongdoing, but not an ounce of proof for anything. His years in law enforcement had taught him that the simplest explanation was usually the right one . . . but there were always exceptions that proved the rule.

He pondered on the situation all the way into Timber City. Once they arrived, he was too busy to think about it very much. Wing kept him hopping as they gathered their supplies and loaded them into the back of the wagon. The barbed wire was at the depot, having come in on a freight from back East. The talkative ticket agent noticed Longarm hefting the rolls of wire and tossing them into the back of the Diamond K wagon, and he strolled out of the building to say, "See you got a job."

"Yep," said Longarm. "Riding for the Diamond K."

"Well, good luck to you."

Longarm waved at the man, then, when he was finished with the barbed wire, told Wing, "I'm going down to the hotel to pick up my gear."

"Ver' good. Start back to ranch soon."

"I'll be right back," Longarm promised.

The desk clerk at the Ponderosa House was the same one who had told Longarm to wipe his feet a couple of days ear-

53

lier. He looked at Longarm and said, "Well. I didn't know if we'd see you back here or not."

"I paid for two nights," Longarm reminded him. "That means my warbag and Winchester ought to still be up in my room."

"Actually, they're here behind the counter. I had one of the boys bring them down earlier this morning."

Longarm supposed the clerk had been within his rights to do that, but it still annoyed him a little. He gave the clerk a curt nod as the man handed the rifle and the warbag over the counter to him.

"Leaving town, are you?" asked the clerk.

"I'm riding for the Diamond K now," said Longarm. Wouldn't hurt to spread that news, he thought. Having a job in the area would allow him to poke around without arousing any suspicions—he hoped.

He had to get word to Aurora McEntire that he was still working on her behalf, despite his employment on Matt Kinsman's ranch. The best thing to do might be to pay a surreptitious visit to the lumber camp as soon as possible. He would keep his eyes open for an opportunity to do just that.

He slung his warbag over his shoulder and carried the Winchester back down to the depot, where Wing was waiting impatiently on the seat of the spring wagon. The reins were already in the cook's hands when Longarm tossed his warbag in the back on top of the supplies. He kept the rifle across his knees as he settled down on the seat next to Wing.

"Must get back to ranch now," said Wing as he slapped the reins against the backs of the mule team pulling the wagon.

"What's your hurry?" asked Longarm.

"Mr. Kinsman, he want peach cobbler for supper tonight. Take long time get ready and cook."

Longarm's culinary skills began and ended with biscuits, beans, bacon, and a few other items of trail food, so he didn't dispute Wing's statement. All he knew about peach cobbler was that he liked to eat it, not how long it took to prepare it.

Wing kept the wagon moving at a brisk pace as they left town on the trail that ran to the north, roughly paralleling the

54

mountains and twisting among the foothills. Longarm rocked easily with the vehicle's motion.

They had covered about half the distance between Timber City and the Diamond K when Wing hit a particularly rough stretch of trail. Longarm was jolted heavily.

As his head jerked to the side, what sounded like a giant bee whipped past his ear.

Longarm knew that sound, knew it all too well. Hard on the heels of it came the crack of a rifle. Longarm lifted the Winchester and worked its lever, jacking a shell into the chamber, as he called out to Wing, "Whip up those jugheads! Somebody's shooting at us!"

Wing let out a startled yell and began flapping the reins harder. Longarm had no idea where the first shot had come from, but as a second bullet buzzed past his head, he saw a puff of smoke come from a thickly wooded knoll about two hundred yards ahead of them, to the left of the trail. Which meant as the wagon careened along, it was actually drawing closer to the bushwhacker—or bushwhackers, because there might be more than one.

Longarm snapped the Winchester to his shoulder and fired three times as fast as he could work the Winchester's lever. He didn't expect to hit anything—the spring wagon had a gentler ride than a plain buckboard, but he was still bouncing around pretty good—but maybe the return fire would distract the hidden rifleman a little anyway.

A slug chewed splinters from the narrow patch of wagon seat between them, making both of them jump and Wing yell, "Son of a bitch!" Longarm threw another shot at the knoll. The trail was too narrow for the wagon to be able to turn around easily, so the best course of action—the only course of action, really—was to rush straight ahead just like they were doing.

The mules were running flat out now. Mules were sometimes difficult to get started, but once they began running there was no stopping them for a while. Longarm was jolted again, and had to grab the small iron railing around the outside of the seat to keep from being thrown from his perch. Beside him, Wing was still yelling and whipping the mules, though it was no longer really necessary considering the way they were already galloping.

Another sharp crack sounded, but this time it didn't come from a hidden gun. It was much closer, right underneath them, in fact. Longarm recognized it as the sound of an axle breaking. "Look out, Wing!" he yelled as he felt the right front corner of the wagon dip drastically. Then the wheel spun off, and the body of the wagon crashed into the rutted trail.

Longarm kicked himself upward off the seat, trying to throw himself clear. Somehow he managed to hang on to the Winchester as he sailed through the air and then slammed to the ground next to the trail. Luckily, the grass there was thick enough to break his fall, at least slightly. As he rolled over and over, he heard a grinding crash that he knew was the wagon overturning. He came to a stop on his belly and shook his head, trying to clear away some of the cobwebs that had gathered there during the last few perilous seconds.

Wing had jumped clear of the wagon too, Longarm saw. The wiry little Chinaman was scrambling to his feet on the other side of the trail. He darted toward the wreckage of the wagon, clearly intending to use it for cover from the ambusher's fire.

The hidden gunman on the knoll wasn't shooting at Wing, however. His target was Longarm, who surged up onto hands and knees as slugs thudded into the ground around him. He flung himself toward the trail and the overturned wagon, sprawling behind the wrecked vehicle as more lead whined around him.

Wing crawled over next to him, and Longarm said grimly, "You might be safer staying as far away from me as you can, old son. It's me that damned bushwhacker's after."

"Yeah, but it's my wagon that bastard made me wreck!" Wing shot back, his singsong accent vanished now. "Gimme a gun, Custis!"

Longarm didn't have time to ponder the transformation in the cook. He just slid the .44 from the cross-draw rig at his waist and extended it butt-first to Wing. "Pepper the top of that knoll with this," he said. "You can't really reach it from

56

here with a handgun, but maybe it'll keep the son of a bitch occupied for a minute."

"What are you going to do?"

"Try to get behind him." Longarm had already spotted a gully that ran from near the trail to behind the knoll. If he could reach it, he could work his way along it until he might have a shot at the bushwhacker from a different angle.

Wing reached into the pile of supplies that had been tossed helter-skelter from the back of the wagon. He grinned as he brought out a box of .44s. "With these extra cartridges, I can keep that low-down skunk hoppin'!" he promised.

Longarm nodded, then moved to the other end of the wagon and waited in a crouch. Shots were still coming from the knoll, the bullets smacking into the thick wood of the wagon's body but not penetrating. After a moment, Wing raised up enough to stick the barrel of the revolver over the edge of the wagon. He blazed away at the knoll.

At the same instant, Longarm launched himself into a run that carried him toward the beginning of the gully. It was about twenty yards away, and Wing's covering fire allowed Longarm to cover fifteen of those yards before the bushwhacker realized he was in no danger from the handgun. A couple of slugs kicked up clods of dirt around Longarm's feet as he raced for the gully, but all they made him do was run faster. He threw himself forward in a dive that carried him out of the line of fire.

Wing had reloaded and was shooting again. The rifleman couldn't ignore him completely. Accuracy was impossible at that distance with a pistol, but pure dumb luck was always within the realm of possibility. Chance might carry one of Wing's shots that far and pose a danger to the ambusher.

Pushing himself up into a crouch, Longarm ran along the bottom of the gully, using the barrel of the Winchester to thrust aside brush that clawed at him and tried to entangle him. Within moments, he had several painful scratches on his hands and face from the briars. He stuck his head up to see how close he was to the knoll.

He had covered more than half the distance when he became aware that he no longer heard the spiteful crack of the rifle, only the steady booming of the Colt that Wing was using. Having seen Longarm disappear into the gully, the bushwhacker might be playing it safe. He might be headed for his horse at this very moment, intending to flee so that he could try again to ambush Longarm some other time.

Longarm wasn't going to allow that to happen. He increased his pace, ignoring the stubborn brambles.

A couple of minutes later, he emerged from the gully and saw that he was behind the knoll where the rifleman had hidden. He heard the thud of hoofs. There was only one bushwhacker, Longarm saw, and the man was already mounted up and wheeling his horse around, about fifty yards away.

Longarm brought the Winchester to his shoulder and yelled, "Hey!" The bushwhacker twisted in the saddle and tried to bring his own rifle around for a shot, but Longarm pressed the trigger first. The Winchester kicked against his shoulder, and through the haze of powder smoke that spurted from its muzzle, he saw the ambusher go flying from the back of the horse as if he were a puppet being jerked around by a puppeteer in a giant Punch and Judy show. The gunman went one way, his rifle the other, and Longarm was pounding toward the man in a run before either of them hit the ground.

There hadn't been time for any fancy shooting, drat the luck, Longarm thought as he came up to the sprawled body. His bullet had taken the man in the left side and punched clear through to the right, ventilating both lungs and probably the bushwhacker's heart. He was stone dead already, eyes open and glazed.

Longarm had never seen him before.

Hunkered on his heels beside the body, Longarm quickly went through the man's pockets, finding only the makin's and a couple of double eagles. Blood money? Longarm wondered. The bushwhacker wore range clothes, and it was clear from the high-crowned hat that had fallen from his head and the riding boots on his feet that he was no lumberjack. Longarm didn't recall seeing him on the Diamond K—but he might not have seen every one of Kinsman's hands in the time he had been on the ranch. Wing would surely know if this was one of Kinsman's riders, though.

Longarm straightened and walked to the top of the knoll. The gun Wing had been using was silent now, so Longarm shouted, "Hold your fire, Wing! It's me, Custis!" He stepped into sight of the trail and waved the rifle over his head.

Wing emerged from behind the wreckage, and Longarm waved for him to approach. The cook hurried up the slope and asked, "Are you all right?"

"Yeah, but that bushwhacker ain't. I had to kill him." Now that the situation wasn't quite so urgent, Longarm added, "What the hell happened to that accent of yours?"

Wing grinned sheepishly. "I've lived in this country for nearly thirty years, Custis. Came over to San Francisco back in the fifties. Most folks take one look at me, though, and expect me to start waving a hatchet around and talking like a heathen Chinee." He shrugged. "I've found it's usually easier to give folks what they want."

Longarm chuckled and shook his head. "I've run up against some real hatchet men from time to time. You do a passable imitation, Wing. If that's the way you want it, I won't say nothing about it when we get back to the ranch. Right now, I want you to take a look at that fella who just tried to kill us."

Chapter 6

Wing didn't recognize the dead bushwhacker either, and he *did* know all the men who rode for the Diamond K.

"Rough-lookin' gent," he said as he gazed down at the corpse, "but I can tell you this for certain, Custis, I never saw him before."

"Me neither," grunted Longarm. "Wonder why he was trying to kill me."

"Maybe he wanted to steal those supplies we had in the wagon."

"Maybe," Longarm said dubiously. He knew better. He had been the target of enough ambush attempts to realize when someone was trying to gun him down. The dead man hadn't cared about the supplies, or the wagon, or even Wing.

He had just wanted Longarm dead.

They each took one of the bushwhacker's legs and dragged the corpse down the hill to the trail. Then Longarm went back for the man's horse. Once that was done, they set about getting the wagon upright again. The mules hadn't broken their traces and run off, for which Longarm was mighty grateful. He and

Wing unhitched a couple of the animals and tied ropes from them to the wagon. When they got the mules to pull with some yelling and whacking across the rumps, the ropes drew taut and then pulled the wagon back onto its wheels—back onto three wheels anyway, since one had come off. Longarm found it and rolled it back to the spot of the wreck. Then he and Wing replaced the broken axle with the spare that was hung underneath the wagon and put the wheel back on. It was hard, sweaty work, but they got it done. Most of the supplies had spilled out of the vehicle when it overturned. Longarm and Wing gathered them up and replaced them in the bed of the wagon, then added the body of the dead ambusher. Longarm tied the man's horse on behind the wagon.

"They probably expected us to be back on the ranch before now," Wing said as he got the wagon moving once again. "Might be gettin' worried by now."

A few minutes later, he was proven right. A group of riders led by Joe Traywick came trotting around a bend in the trail. Traywick held up his hand in a signal to halt, and the horsemen waited until Wing drove the wagon up to them.

"Where in blazes've you been, Wing?" demanded the foreman. "Figured you'd be back more'n an hour ago."

"We have trouble, Mist' Joe," said Wing, and Longarm tried not to grin at the return of the accent. "Man try shoot us. Wagon turn over."

"What the hell!" exclaimed Traywick.

Longarm jerked a thumb over his shoulder. "Wing's telling the truth of it, Joe," he said. "The ambush sort of backfired on the fella, though. He's back here, dead as a mackerel. Didn't give me no choice but to shoot him."

Traywick prodded his horse forward so that he could look into the back of the wagon. He grunted as he studied the dead man's face. "You know him, Custis?"

"Nope. I was sort of hoping you might've seen him around these parts before."

Traywick shook his head solemnly. "Never saw this buzzard in my life. You reckon it was a holdup?"

Longarm nodded, catching Wing's eye for an instant as he did so. "I reckon he was after our supplies and the wagon.

Could be he saw us loading up in town and rode out to get ahead of us so he could set up his ambush.''

"Well, good riddance." Traywick rubbed his jaw. "There's a deputy sheriff in Timber City. When we get back to the ranch, I'll send a rider to him with word of what happened. He can come out with the undertaker for the body if he wants, or we'll plant the son of a bitch ourselves. Come on. I reckon Matt's gettin' a mite worried about the two of you by now."

Wing gave Longarm a puzzled look as the wagon rolled forward again. Earlier, Longarm had been clear about the bushwhacker wanting to kill him, yet now he was telling a different story. Clearly, Wing was willing to play along with that, but he had to wonder what Longarm was up to.

The Chinese cook was used to keeping a secret of his own, thought Longarm. If he was going to reveal who he was to anyone on the Diamond K, it would be Wing. It might come in handy to have an ally on the ranch—but only if it became absolutely necessary.

When they reached the headquarters of the Diamond K, both Matt Kinsman and his daughter Molly were standing on the front porch of the big ranch house. At the sight of Longarm sitting on the wagon, Molly hurried down off the porch as if she was going to run out to meet them, then stopped abruptly. Kinsman strode past her and demanded, "What the hell happened? How come it took you so long to get back from town?"

Wing answered the questions. "Badman ambush us, Mist' Kinsman. Try kill us and steal wagon and supplies."

"The hell you say! Who'd do a thing like that? One of those damn lumberjacks, more'n likely!"

Longarm shook his head. "This fella was no lumberjack," he said, inclining his head toward the back of the wagon. "Here's his body, if you want to take a look at him, Boss. None of us know who he was."

As Kinsman came over to the wagon to peer at the corpse in the back, he asked, "That the son of a bitch's horse tied up there?"

"Yep," said Traywick. "The brand on it ain't one from around here, if that's what you're thinkin', Matt. Looks like this fella was just a drifter who picked the wrong gents to bushwhack.''

Kinsman's rugged face was impassive as he studied the dead man without a sign of recognition. "Which one of you killed him?''

"I did,'' said Longarm.

"That was good shootin'. Either of you hurt?''

Molly had come closer to the wagon, and Longarm saw her watching intently. He said, "Nope, just shaken up a mite,'' and saw a look of relief appear in her eyes. Of course, he reminded himself, she could have been worried about Wing, who had evidently been with Kinsman for quite a while. Just because she was glad neither of them had been hurt didn't necessarily mean she was getting attached to *him*.

Traywick dismounted and led his horse over to Kinsman. "I'll send a rider into town to tell the deputy about all this, Matt,'' he said. "Pretty clear-cut case of self-defense, if you ask me.''

"Damn right it is,'' said Kinsman with a snort. "Diamond K riders don't kill folks without a good reason, even owlhoots like this one.'' He jerked his head toward the rear of the house. "Wing, take that wagon on around back and get it unloaded.'' Kinsman looked around, and his gaze fell on one of the young cowboys standing nearby. "Seth, go help Wing.''

Seth Thomas's eyes widened. "But that's *his* job!'' he said, pointing at Longarm.

"Custis has done enough for one day, downin' that bushwhacker like that,'' snapped Kinsman. "Now get movin', boy. Custis, you come on inside with me. I want to hear more about this.''

Longarm tried hard not to grin at Seth as he stepped down from the wagon and retrieved his warbag from the back. He was still carrying the Winchester. Seth was red-faced and fuming, but he did as Kinsman had told him to do, following the wagon toward the rear of the house as Wing drove it away.

Longarm went into the house with Kinsman, Molly, and Traywick. The rancher led the way to his study, and as he paused before the door he said, "Go help Wing in the kitchen, Molly.''

"Why?" she demanded. "Because I'm just a helpless female and hadn't ought to listen to you talking about men getting killed?"

"That's right," said Kinsman. "That's just exactly right."

Molly's eyes narrowed angrily, but Traywick moved smoothly between her and her father and said quietly, "Best do like Matt says, Molly."

She sighed in resignation. "Oh, all right, Joe. I'll go along with the old goat . . . for your sake."

"Old goat, is it?" exclaimed Kinsman indignantly. "Why, you little—"

Molly turned with a flounce—not an easy thing to do while wearing jeans and a man's shirt, thought Longarm—and walked away down the hall, ignoring her father's reprimand.

Kinsman shook his head. "Gal's got a mind of her own," he muttered. "Come on, Custis. I want you to tell me everything that happened."

Longarm did so, leaving out only his conviction that the ambusher had been after him and him alone. As he talked, he lit a cheroot, and both Kinsman and Traywick filled pipes and lit them.

When Longarm was finished, Kinsman blew out a cloud of smoke and said, "Sorry this had to happen to you on just your second day here, Custis. On the other hand, maybe you got your bad luck out of the way early."

"Don't seem like bad luck to me," said Longarm with a shake of his head. "I'm still breathing, and the other gent ain't."

Kinsman chuckled. "You could sure as hell look at it that way, all right." His expression became more serious. "Say, I wonder if it was that McEntire woman or one of her men who hired that fella to bushwhack you?"

Longarm frowned. Kinsman was bound and determined to blame everything that went wrong on the loggers. "Don't recall saying that I thought anybody hired the fella," he pointed out. "Seemed to me like a simple holdup."

"Could've been," said Kinsman, nodding slowly. "Or maybe not."

Unfortunately, the rancher was right. Though Longarm

didn't agree with Kinsman's eagerness to cast blame on the McEntire timber outfit, that didn't mean Kinsman was incorrect in his assumptions. While Aurora had given no indication that she was the type to strike back at an enemy by hiring a gunman, Longarm didn't know her well enough to completely rule out the possibility. Of course, if she *was* responsible for this attack, that meant she was trying to play him for a fool by asking for his help, then continuing to make the conflict between cattlemen and loggers worse.

Wouldn't be the first time he had run across a woman who figured her pretty face would allow her to pull everybody's strings, he reminded himself. Under the circumstances, it was even more important that he find a chance to talk to Aurora McEntire again, and soon.

The chance came sooner than he expected. As dinner was being completed that night, the rider Joe Traywick had sent to Timber City to inform the local deputy of what had happened reappeared, and with him came the star packer himself. The deputy sheriff was a red-faced, big-bellied man in a town suit and derby hat. He revealed a sun-freckled, mostly bald pate when he took off the derby to nod respectfully to Molly. After a longing glance at the spread of food Wing had prepared, the man turned to Kinsman and said in a high-pitched voice, "I'm sorry, Mr. Kinsman, but I got to ask you to let that cowboy called Custis come back to town with me."

Longarm sat up straighter in surprise. Kinsman nodded toward him and said to the deputy, "There he is, Bullfinch. Ask him yourself."

Deputy Bullfinch—as the target of more than one humorous comment about his own name, Longarm didn't envy the local lawman—turned to him and said, "How about it, mister?"

"What do you need me for?" asked Longarm coolly.

"The sheriff says I got to start doin' things more legal-like. That means havin' a inquest ever' time somebody gets themselves killed by violent means."

Longarm didn't point out that it might be difficult to kill somebody by non-violent means. Bullfinch's request tied right in with Longarm's own plans, so he nodded and said, "Sure, I'll be glad to come with you, Deputy."

"I'm much obliged. The hearin' will be tomorrow mornin' at nine o'clock. You can stay the night in the Ponderosa House, or if you like, there's nobody in the cell at the jail house right now, so you could sleep there."

Kinsman spoke up again. "No rider of mine is spendin' the night in jail unless he deserves it. I'll pay for your room at the hotel, Custis."

"Thanks, Boss," said Longarm with a grin. "I got to admit, the idea of sleeping behind bars don't appeal much to me, even if the door isn't locked."

Seth Thomas put in, "Bet you've spent more than one night in jail."

"If I have, it's none of your business, junior," Longarm replied crisply.

"That's enough, you two," said Kinsman. He waved a hand at the table, which had plenty of leftovers scattered on it. "Unless you're in a big hurry, Bullfinch, sit down and have some supper before you start back to Timber City."

The deputy practically licked his lips as he reached for an empty chair. "Thanks, Mr. Kinsman," he said eagerly. "I reckon the trip back can wait a spell. That'll give Custis a chance to get together any gear he might want to take."

"That's right," said Longarm dryly. There wasn't much he planned to take along, however. He would be traveling light on this trip to Timber City.

And on the way back, he would pay a visit to the lumber camp and try to find out if maybe, just maybe, Aurora McEntire knew anything about bushwhackers.

The inquest was pretty cut and dried. The local undertaker also served as the coroner, and he swore in a jury of six townies who heard Longarm testify that he had killed the deceased only after the fella had done his best to kill both Longarm and Matt Kinsman's cook, Wing. Deputy Bullfinch had explained to Longarm that Wing wouldn't need to testify, being a Chinaman and all. Longarm's word was good enough for the jury.

The verdict was a foregone conclusion: The deceased had

met his end in the course of committing a crime, so good riddance. Longarm stood up as the coroner banged a gavel on the table in the front room of the undertaking parlor, where the hearing had taken place. "This hearing is adjourned," said the undertaker in a reedy voice.

Longarm turned to Deputy Bullfinch. "You through with me?"

"I reckon so. Appreciate you comin' in with me, Custis. We're tryin' to bring law an' order to this part o' the country, and the only way to do that is to see that ever'thing's done legal-like."

Longarm refrained from commenting that if Bullfinch really wanted to do something for law and order around Timber City, he would have gotten to the bottom of this feud between the cattlemen and the loggers before now. The Justice Department, in the form of Longarm himself, had been called in only when it became obvious that local authorities weren't going to put a stop to the trouble.

Longarm settled his hat on his head and stuck a cheroot in his mouth as he stepped out of the undertaking parlor. His saddlebags and the Winchester were at the hotel, his saddle and the roan at the livery stable. It took only a few minutes to gather everything he needed and ride out of Timber City.

He followed the main trail to the cutoff that led to the lumber camp, and veered west on the smaller path. A few minutes later, one of the lumberjacks stepped out of the underbrush and challenged him. It was similar to his experience the first time he'd come up there. "I'm Deputy Marshal Long," he told the sentry. "I was up here to see Mrs. McEntire a few days ago."

The lumberjack nodded. "Yeah, I remember you. You were in camp the day that boom got away and wrecked Miz McEntire's cabin."

"That's right. I need to speak to her again."

"Go on ahead," the man said with a wave of his hand as he lowered his rifle. "I'll signal for the others to let you pass."

"Much obliged." Longarm prodded the roan into a walk.

As he rode on up the mountain, he spotted several other sentries. He wondered if there had been any more trouble since the runaway boom. Anybody who wanted to sneak up on these loggers was going to have to be pretty stealthy about it now.

When he reached the camp, he saw to his surprise that another log cabin had been thrown up near the sawmill. It was not as large as the one that had been destroyed by the boom, nor did it have a front porch, but it would serve just fine as the camp's headquarters and Aurora's residence. One thing they had plenty of around here, reflected Longarm, was logs.

He swung down from the roan and tied it to the hitching post in front of the newly constructed cabin. Before he could knock on the door, it opened and Aurora stepped out. "I saw you coming, Marshal," she said. "How are you?"

"Reckon I'm fine," replied Longarm. "Any more problems around here?"

"Not so far, thank goodness." Aurora wore a dark blue dress and had a ribbon of the same shade tied in her thick dark hair. "Come inside."

Something about her tone struck Longarm as being cooler than it had been a few days earlier on his previous visit. Could be she was angry he hadn't gotten back out to the camp before now, he told himself. If that was the case, she would likely change her mind once she found out what he had been doing.

However, he realized a moment later that she already knew what he'd been up to—or at least she *thought* she did.

As soon as he had shut the door behind him, she rounded on him and said frostily, "I hear you've gone to work for the enemy."

Longarm's eyes widened a little in surprise. "What—oh, you mean you've heard about how I'm riding for the Diamond K."

"I thought you worked for the government."

"I do," he told her solemnly. "You ever hear of working in secret, Mrs. McEntire?"

She flushed, and he wasn't sure if it was from anger or embarrassment. "You mean you're trying to find proof that Kinsman is behind our trouble?"

"Kinsman—or somebody else on his ranch."

Aurora lowered her eyes. "I'm sorry, Marshal. I should have known it was something like that when I heard in town

68

that you were working for Kinsman. He doesn't know you're a lawman?"

"Nope. I'm not sure how long I can keep it that way, though, so I want to sort out this mess as quick as I can."

"What's to sort out? Just get the proof that he's trying to ruin me and arrest him."

Longarm shook his head. "It ain't quite that easy. For one thing, I'm not completely convinced that Kinsman's to blame for your troubles."

"What?" She stared at him in disbelief. "Who else could it be?"

"I don't rightly know," admitted Longarm. "Could be some of the young punchers on his spread, acting on their own."

"No," insisted Aurora. "That unpleasant old man is behind things, I'm sure of it."

"Or . . . it might be somebody else entirely. Do you have any other enemies who might want to see you have trouble with that government contract?"

"Of course not. It has to be Kinsman," Aurora said stubbornly.

"Funny thing," said Longarm, though he didn't really consider it amusing at all. "He says the same thing about you. He blames you for rustling cattle and poisoning wells on the Diamond K."

Aurora's face lit up again, and this time it was definitely caused by anger. "The old . . . the old fool! How could he think that?"

"He found you and your men cooking steaks the day after some of his cows disappeared," Longarm pointed out. "Don't recollect you mentioning that to me the last time I was out here."

"Because it's such an absurd idea that I didn't think it was worth mentioning!" Aurora crossed her arms across her ample bosom and began to stalk back and forth across the room. Most of her belongings from the other cabin had been salvaged from the wreckage, but this new place was still more sparsely furnished than the original. In addition, it had only one big room, and in one corner was the bed. Aurora's pacing brought her almost to it before she turned back each time. Her self-control slipped, and she began to wave her arms as she said, "I don't understand it! I'm the one whose men have been killed, whose business has been threatened! Kinsman is the one behind it, and you're defending him!"

Longarm felt a surge of anger himself. He had explained his actions. More than that, he had pointed out where Aurora herself had not been completely honest with him. He had as much right to be put out as she did.

Acting on impulse, he stepped forward and caught hold of one of her wrists as she swung her arm through the air. "Wait just a minute!" he said. "I ain't defending anybody. I'm just trying to get to the truth."

"Let go of me, damn you!" She thrust her face up toward his, glaring at him. "You've got no right—"

Longarm was tired of listening to her. He shut her up the best way he knew how.

He kissed her.

His mouth came down hard and demanding on hers. His arms went around her and pulled her against him. Her breasts pressed softly against his chest, flattening as he embraced her. Longarm slid one hand down to the small of her back and massaged the hollow there. Aurora's hands caught hold of his shirt and plucked at it as she moaned deep in her throat.

For a long moment they stood there like that, sharing the hot wet urgency of their mouths. Then Aurora pulled her head away from Longarm's. "We . . . we shouldn't be doing this," she practically gasped.

"You're probably right," Longarm said quietly. He didn't let go of her, however. Instead he lifted a hand and cupped her left breast, feeling the hard nubbin of puckered flesh at its center.

"Oh . . . to hell with it!" exclaimed Aurora breathlessly. "All the men are either up in the woods or working in the mill, and they won't bother us." She reached down to his groin and found the hardness pressing urgently at his denim trousers. "Oh, my!" Her fingers fairly flew over the buttons, and within seconds she had freed his shaft from his pants and his long-handled underwear. Her eyes widened as she closed

70

her hand around the long, thick pole of rock-hard flesh. "It ... it's been such a long time. . . ."

"No need to wait anymore," Longarm said gently. He bent, slipped an arm behind her knees, and scooped her up in his arms. Moving as effortlessly as if she were weightless, he carried her to the bed and lowered her onto the thick, quilted comforter.

His own fingers were pretty damned nimble as he unfastened the buttons on her dress, he thought, especially since all the while she was reaching up and caressing his manhood, fisting her hand around it and running her soft palm up and down the length of him. The way she was licking her lips was downright distracting too. But within a few moments, he had the dress spread open and was pushing up the cotton shift she wore underneath it, revealing firm calves and creamy thighs. As the thick triangle of dark, fine-spun hair at the juncture of her legs came into view, she spread herself wide, and Longarm reached down to the hot, wet core of her. She cried out softly as he fondled her, his fingers exploring the folds of flesh he found between her legs. Her hips thrust up involuntarily as he plunged his middle finger into her.

Mouth half open, eyes glazed with passion, she humped up at him as he caressed her intimately. "D-damn you, Marshal!" she gasped at him. "D-don't just . . . play with me! I need you inside me!"

Longarm was always pretty much glad to oblige a request like that. He withdrew his finger, making her moan in frustration, and shucked his boots and pants as quickly as he could. "Leave the damn shirt on!" said Aurora. "I can't wait!"

Longarm moved over her, and she grasped his pole eagerly to guide it into her. He didn't need much help. Her portal was gaping wide and drenched in her vital juices. Longarm felt the tip of his shaft touch the wetness and surged forward with his hips, burying his full length in her. He was afraid from the way her eyes went so wide that she was going to let out a yell, but she managed to stifle her cry of ecstasy. He held himself there, with Aurora penetrated to the fullest extent, before launching into a steady rhythm of thrusts. She moaned and clutched at him, and her legs came up and locked together at the ankles above his back.

He had to admit that she gave as good as she got, thrusting back at him so that their bellies came together with soft slapping sounds. Each time they came together so that she was filled to the brim, she squeezed him tightly with a surprisingly muscular grip. Though he had been pounding into her for only a short time, he felt his climax threatening to surge up from inside him.

Aurora must have sensed that, because she said hoarsely, "Don't hold back! Give it to me! Fill me up!"

Longarm did just that, tightening his arms around her as his hips drove forward one final time. Then he held himself motionless as his seed boiled out into her in spurt after wrenching spurt. Aurora spasmed too, her own flood mixing with his. Longarm gave one last shudder, then threw his head back and drew a deep breath into his lungs. Below him, Aurora trembled once or twice. Her eyes were closed now, and she was breathing as hard as he was. A fine sheen of sweat covered both of them.

Longarm felt his softening shaft slip out of her. She made a little noise of regret as he rolled to the side. Then she turned her head, opened her eyes, looked at him, and said once again, "Oh, my."

Too out of breath to speak, Longarm settled for lifting a hand to stroke her cheek.

"That was ... that was so wonderful," she said. "I ... I haven't been with a man since ... since Angus died. I ... I had almost forgotten what it was like."

"It comes back to you," Longarm managed to say.

"Yes, it does," agreed Aurora. She reached down and stroked the instrument that had given her such pleasure. "Oh, yes, it surely does!"

Chapter 7

The way Aurora kept playing with him, Longarm figured he was going to be ready for some more loving pretty soon, but after a few minutes, she sat up suddenly and said, "Do you hear that?"

Longarm was so caught up in the sensuous pleasure she had been giving him that for a second he didn't hear anything except the pounding of his pulse in his head. Then he realized that it wasn't his pulse alone he was hearing.

There were the hoofbeats of an approaching horse outside the cabin, hoofbeats that came to an abrupt halt.

Aurora swung her legs out of bed and stood up, tugging her shift down around her hips and frantically fastening the buttons on her dress. The wanton female of a few moments before had disappeared, and the respectable businesswoman and widow was quickly coming once more to the forefront. She hurried to one of the oilcloth-covered windows and moved the oilcloth aside just enough to peer out. There was a startled expression on her face as she swung back toward Longarm.

"It's Ben Callahan!" she hissed. "You've got to get out of here!"

Seeing how she was reacting to the prospect of company, Longarm had already reached for his clothes. While he felt a little resentful about her attitude, not to mention a mite embarrassed at the way this encounter had suddenly turned into something out of a French farce, he didn't want to cause trouble for Aurora. If she wanted him out, he would do his best to oblige. He finished buttoning up his pants and stomped into his boots, then snagged his gunbelt from the back of the chair next to the bed where he had hung it.

The cabin had only the one door, but there was a good-sized window in the back. Longarm moved the oilcloth covering aside and swung a leg over the sill. He paused and looked back at Aurora, who was running a comb through her disheveled hair and pinning it back in place. The transformation was well nigh miraculous. She didn't look like she'd ever had an impure thought, and there was certainly no hint of what she had actually been doing with him on that bed a few minutes earlier. As Longarm watched, she gave a quick jerk to the comforter, which straightened it out and removed the evidence of their activities.

Longarm caught her eye and mouthed "So long" at her. For a second she looked exasperated, as if she wished he would go on and leave and be done with it, but then she gave him a quick grin that told him she had enjoyed their love-making every bit as much as he had. Carrying the memory of that grin with him, Longarm stepped out the window and let the oilcloth fall back into place behind him.

Then he paused just outside the cabin and thought about what Aurora had said. According to her, the visitor was Ben Callahan, and it took only a second for Longarm to figure out why that name sounded so familiar. Callahan owned the logging outfit that was operating to the north of the McEntire timber lease in the Cascades.

And for some reason, Aurora didn't want Callahan to even suspect that she had been enjoying a midday romp with a man. Otherwise she would have told Longarm to get dressed but would have allowed him to remain in the cabin while she

74

greeted Callahan. She could have introduced him to the owner of the other timber company and come up with a plausible reason for his being there.

Clearly, that hadn't even occurred to her, and Longarm wondered why.

There was one way to find out, he thought. Given an opportunity to eavesdrop, he wasn't going to pass it up. There was no way of knowing when something he overheard might turn out to be important to the case.

Those thoughts went through Longarm's head in a flash. Leaning closer to the window, he heard the sharp rapping on the door, then heard it open and Aurora say, "Why, Ben Callahan! What are you doing here?" Her voice was pleasant enough, but it held an undercurrent of tension.

A man's voice said harshly, "You know perfectly well why I'm here, Aurora. I've come to raise my offer—though I warn you this is the last time I'll do so. Forty thousand dollars, and not a penny more."

"Don't be ridiculous, Ben," said Aurora. "That government contract alone is worth twenty or thirty times that much, not to mention the lumber I've been able to sell to private business. Why should I sell you my company for forty thousand dollars?"

"Because it's all the cash I've got in the world," said Ben Callahan, "and because we both know that contract should have been mine!"

"We both had a chance to bid on it," Aurora returned firmly.

"Yes, but you took advantage of the fact that Angus and I were friends and used to be partners! You found out what I was going to bid, and then you undercut me!"

Aurora's voice was a smooth but dangerous purr as she said, "You and Angus were never friends from the day you dissolved the partnership, Ben. You thought you could do better on your own, and when you found out that you couldn't, you held it against Angus and resented him for the rest of his life."

Heavy footsteps stomped back and forth across the floor. Callahan was pacing angrily, Longarm thought. Longarm put his face close to the window and risked a quick glance through

75

the narrow gap around the oilcloth. He was grateful that the sawmill and the cookshack were on the other side of the cabin. If anybody saw him peeping into the window like this, he'd feel like a damned fool.

And yet he wanted a look at Ben Callahan, and he got one as the rival timber magnate swung around to stalk back across the cabin's single room. Callahan was a tall, broad-shouldered man who looked like he had swung an ax and wielded a saw plenty of times himself. His features were craggy, battered, and at the moment flushed. He was balding, and the hair that was left was brown laced with gray. The muscles of his arms and shoulders bulged the coat of the tweed suit he wore.

"That's not true," he answered Aurora's accusation. "I never resented Angus or envied his success."

Longarm didn't even know the man, and even *he* doubted the truth of that claim. Callahan sounded as if he had resented Angus McEntire plenty.

"Well, I'll certainly not sell the company to you," said Aurora. "Poor Angus would turn over in his grave if I did that. But I *will* buy you out if you'd care to sell."

"What?" roared Callahan. "By God, woman, if I didn't know better, I'd say Angus passed his brass balls on to you when he died!"

Outside the cabin, Longarm had to suppress a chuckle. Though he knew Callahan was deadly serious, something about the idea of Aurora McEntire with brass balls just struck Longarm as funny. He gritted his teeth to keep from laughing and continued eavesdropping.

"This is getting us nowhere," Aurora said coldly. "I want you to leave, Ben. I'm not interested in selling my company to you now, nor will I be in the future."

Ominously, Callahan said, "I wouldn't be so sure about that. Everybody in this part of the country knows you've been having trouble, Aurora. You might be better off to salvage what profit you can by selling and get out now, before anybody else gets hurt."

Longarm stiffened. Of all the high-handed . . . ! This put things in a whole new light, he thought. Callahan was blatantly threatening Aurora, practically admitting that he was behind her troubles. Longarm had been looking for another suspect in this case—and he had just found one.

"I won't stand for that kind of talk," snapped Aurora. Longarm heard the rasp of a drawer opening in a desk. "Get out."

"You might as well put that down, Aurora," said Callahan. "I'm not afraid of you. You're not going to shoot me."

Longarm sure as hell hoped not. He didn't want to have to bust in there and take a gun away from Aurora if she was mad enough to plug Callahan.

The next instant, he heard the unmistakable metallic clicking of a pistol's hammer being drawn back and cocked. "You think I won't?" Aurora asked. "I'll shoot you, Ben. I promise you, I'll be glad to shoot you."

Clearly, this was a long-standing disagreement between these two. If they got along this badly, Longarm thought, why hadn't Aurora said anything when he'd asked her if she had any other enemies? From the sounds of everything going on in that cabin, Ben Callahan sure as hell fit the bill.

"All right, I'm going," Callahan growled after a moment. "But this isn't over, Aurora. One of these days, you're going to come to your senses."

"Not if it means selling my company to you. Now, get out of here. Good-bye, Ben."

Longarm heard some more muttering from Callahan. Then the door of the cabin opened and shut. He heard Callahan stomp around a little before a horse trotted off. Callahan hadn't gone graciously.

The oilcloth over the window was pushed aside, and Aurora said, "You can come back in now, Marshal."

"After what we've been through together, you ought to call me Custis," Longarm told her as he climbed in through the window. "And how'd you know I was still out here? I could have sneaked off."

"I just figured you waited to hear what was going to happen. I never saw a lawman who wasn't curious."

Longarm grinned. "Guilty as charged. And Callahan may be too."

"What do you mean by that?" asked Aurora.

"I mean, didn't it ever occur to you that maybe Callahan is the one who's hurting your operation? It makes more sense than blaming everything on Kinsman and the Diamond K. Callahan and his men would know a lot more about how to ruin things for loggers than a bunch of cowboys would."

Aurora shook her head. "That's ridiculous. Ben would never do such a thing, regardless of any hostility he might feel toward me. He's too much of a gentleman."

Longarm suppressed a snort of disbelief. From what he had seen and heard of the man, Callahan wouldn't stop at anything to get what he wanted—and what he wanted now was the McEntire Timber Company.

"Did I hear you say that Callahan and your husband used to be partners?"

"Years ago," Aurora replied with a nod. "Before I even married Angus, in fact. Then, when he and I became engaged, I think that Ben seemed to regard it as a . . . a betrayal of sorts. He said he was going to form his own company and go his own way. Angus tried to talk him out of it, but there was no persuading Ben to change his mind." She smiled wistfully. "I don't think Ben likes me very much, and I always felt a little guilty about driving a wedge between him and Angus. They were good friends, good partners, before that."

"Maybe you're letting that blind you to the fact that Callahan could be behind your troubles," Longarm told her. "Guilt can make you see things differently."

Aurora laughed quietly. "I don't feel *that* guilty. I loved Angus very much, and I've never regretted marrying him, no matter what other circumstances might have arisen from that. I just don't think Ben is capable of such violence."

Longarm wasn't convinced. He and Aurora might have to agree to disagree on that point for the time being, however. He couldn't make a move against either Kinsman or Callahan without coming up with some proof first, solid evidence that not even Aurora could dispute.

At least he had another lead now, despite his lack of progress so far on the Diamond K.

And that was where he needed to go now. Kinsman, Traywick, and the others were expecting him to come straight back to the ranch after the inquest in Timber City, and he had already delayed long enough. It had been a mighty pleasurable delay, of course, and maybe informative as well.

"I've got to be riding," he told Aurora.

"Back to Kinsman's ranch?"

"That's right."

"Even though you don't believe he's guilty?"

"I never said that," Longarm pointed out. "I said I wasn't completely convinced, that I hadn't found any proof either way just yet. That doesn't mean I'm going to stop looking."

But he was going to be looking long and hard at Ben Callahan too, he added to himself.

As he started to turn away, Aurora stopped him by placing a hand on his arm. Her gaze was soft and warm as she looked at him and said, "Be careful, Custis. We may not agree about everything, but you've already done so much for me." She stepped forward and lifted her face to his for a brief kiss.

Longarm knew what she meant. He had reawakened a passion inside her that had been slumbering since the death of her husband. She had submerged herself in work, the business that had been built by Angus McEntire. Longarm had brought her out of that for a few minutes, lifting her back to the surface so that she had emerged into the glorious sunlight of her own needs and desires. The hot urgency of her kiss made it clear that she was eagerly anticipating the next opportunity to repeat the experience—as was Longarm.

But for now he had his own business to tend to, so after a final embrace, he left the cabin without looking back and untied his horse's reins from the hitching post. Swinging up into the roan's saddle, he pointed the animal down the path that would take him back to the main trail. As he rode past the cookshack, the bald-headed old biscuit-shooter stepped out and lifted a hand in greeting. Longarm returned the wave, then put the lumber camp behind him.

He didn't see the sentries on his way back to the main trail. They had withdrawn into the timber to stand guard in case anyone bent on trouble tried to approach the camp. Of course, watching the trail was one thing, and Longarm didn't blame the loggers for posting sentries. But there were other ways to approach the camp, and they couldn't all be watched, not if any work had to get done. He felt a tingle of uneasiness. Other than the bushwhack attempt on his life, the last couple of days had been free of trouble.

That couldn't last, thought Longarm. Every instinct he had developed over a lot of dangerous years as a lawman told him so.

Still, he wasn't expecting all hell to break loose quite so quickly. . . .

He swung his mount back onto the main trail, then a few minutes later veered off it again when he came to the path leading to the headquarters of the Diamond K. This path led through a thick stand of timber, and though the day was sunny, the shadows were thick here underneath the boughs of the towering pines. Longarm breathed the fragrant air and thought about what he had learned today. He was convinced that Ben Callahan was a plausible suspect in Aurora's troubles.

The volley of shots that ripped out of the trees to his right drove those thoughts from his mind and replaced them with the need for sheer survival. The bullets drove him from the saddle too, as one of the slugs ripped across his back, plowing a shallow furrow in the flesh and clipping his left shoulder blade. With a cry of pain, he twisted and tumbled from the roan's back, barely thinking to kick his feet free of the stirrups as he fell.

The roan bolted forward, breaking into a startled gallop. Longarm heard the pounding of its hoofbeats mixed with the sharp crackle of gunfire as he thudded heavily to the ground. Even hurting as he was, he kept his wits about him and rolled toward the far side of the trail as fast as he could. He was aware of bullets smacking into the ground around him, but as far as he could tell, none of them struck him. So far, the wound he had suffered in the first volley was his only injury.

Of course, that was enough, he thought as he slid down the narrow grassy verge along the edge of the trail. The crease across his back burned like blazes, and pain shot through his upper torso every time he moved. Still, he knew he had to hunt some cover in a hurry, or within a few moments he wouldn't be hurting at all.

He'd be too dead for that.

A deadfall lay some ten yards away. Longarm palmed out his Colt, which thankfully had not fallen from its holster when he tumbled off the horse, and began triggering as fast as he could as he came up in a crouch. The shots were directed toward the blank face of the woods across the trail, where the other shots had come from. He had no real hopes of hitting anything; he just wanted to distract the sons of bitches while he scampered for some shelter.

The strategy worked. A couple of shots came his way as he dashed for the fallen tree, but neither of them were close. Longarm threw himself forward and sprawled behind the log. The tree had been a good-sized one, with a trunk several feet in diameter. None of the bushwhackers' slugs were going to reach him as long as he stayed behind the deadfall.

There was more than one hidden rifleman this time. Longarm was convinced of that. He had heard the sound of at least three separate rifles. He grimaced as he began thumbing fresh shells into the Colt. Even though he was safe enough for the moment, they still had him in a damned bad spot. If they had plenty of ammunition, they could wait him out. Or some of them could just work around behind him and catch him in a cross fire. He was pinned down good and proper.

The gunmen were still firing—he could hear the crack of their rifles and the thud of bullets hitting the log—but their attack was more desultory now. They wanted him dead, but they weren't in any big hurry about it.

Longarm felt the sticky wetness of his blood soaking the shirt on his back. He didn't think he was losing blood fast enough for that to be a real concern. Chances were, the bushwhackers would get tired and rush him to get it over with before he ever had a chance to bleed to death.

He looked around, searching for something that might offer him a way out of this dilemma. The bushwhackers had picked the spot well for their ambush. In many places along this trail, the woods came almost right up to the path, so that a rider could have reached out and brushed his fingers along the rough bark of the trunks. On the other side of the trail, where the riflemen lurked, that was the case. On *this* side, however, there was a clearing behind the spot where Longarm lay. The edge of the pine forest was a good twenty feet away. If he tried to stand up and run into the shelter of the trees, or even attempted to crawl across the clearing, the would-be killers would have no trouble picking him off. It was pure luck that they hadn't done worse than wing him so far.

With nothing in his surroundings offering any hope, Longarm turned his attention to the thing closest to him: the log. The tree had been well over a hundred feet tall when it was alive, and he was lying near the base of it. Craning his neck, he looked along the length of the fallen tree and saw that the far end was rotten and collapsed on itself. Disease had claimed this giant, not the woodsman's ax. That was why it had been left lying here. No doubt it was rotten clear through, useless for lumber.

In fact, there was a good-sized hole in the trunk a few feet from him, and as Longarm looked at it, an idea began to form in his head. He crawled over to the hole, wincing as the squirming motion made his wounded back spasm in agony.

The opening in the trunk was only about a foot wide. Longarm grasped the edges of it and crumbled them away in fist-sized pieces. As he had thought, the tree was mostly rotten. When he had widened the hole enough for him to stick his head into it, he took a deep breath and did so, twisting his neck so that he could look toward the far end of the deadfall.

Light. He saw light.

Small animals had gotten into the tree and hollowed it out at some time in the past, making a den of it. Longarm could still smell a faint, gamy odor, a legacy of whatever creature had made its home here. The varmint could still be up in there, he supposed, but with all the shooting going on, that was doubtful. Any critter with sense would have already headed for the tall and uncut.

No, there was probably nothing in that log except grub-worms and other crawling varmints. The thought of joining them made the skin on the back of Longarm's neck prickle uncomfortably.

He might not have any choice, however. If those bushwhackers had a lick of sense, they would be working their way around behind him even now.

He dug his clasp knife out of his pants pocket and unfolded the blade. Then, with the knife and with his bare hand, he began enlarging the hole in the log. It would have to be pretty big to accommodate his broad shoulders. Ignoring the pain in his back, he worked feverishly. The hidden riflemen wouldn't have as much time as he had first thought, he realized. Those shots might be heard at the logging camp, and some of Aurora's men might come to investigate.

Unless those bushwhackers *worked* for Aurora McEntire.

Longarm didn't want to think about that possibility. It was never pleasant to ponder that a woman he had recently bedded with such pleasing results for both of them would try to have him killed, but it had happened before and could again. Suspicion was just an occupational hazard, like getting shot at, but that didn't mean he had to like either one of them.

When he judged that the opening was large enough, he wiggled his head and shoulders inside. His shoulders scraped a little on the sides, but they made it. Using his hands and his toes to push himself along, he began making his laborious way toward the irregular circle of light that marked the far end of the log.

He wasn't the only thing crawling in this log, as he had expected. Gritting his teeth, Longarm ignored the many-legged touches of the insects that scampered over him. Ants stung him until he thought he was going to bellow in a combination of anger and fiery pain. His wounded back dragged against the top of the log, and he knew he was damaging it even worse.

The price he was paying might well be worth it, though, because when he was a little more than halfway to the far end of the log, he heard a voice yell, "Hold your fire! He ain't over here!"

A grim smile plucked at Longarm's mouth. As he had expected, at least one of the bushwhackers had circled the deadfall and come at it from the other direction, from the clearing. And as far as they could tell, their intended quarry had vanished. Longarm had scattered the chunks of rotten wood he'd cut away and torn from the hole in the log, and there was enough litter on the forest floor that he hoped the signs of what he had done would not be too readily apparent.

"What do you mean he's not there?" came another voice. "The star-packin' bastard's *got* to be there! We saw him run behind that deadfall, and he never came out!"

"I don't care, he's gone."

The hollowed-out passage inside the log suddenly narrowed down, and Longarm felt his shoulders pinched. No matter how hard he shoved with his toes, he couldn't make any progress. What if he got *stuck* in here? That was a chilling thought.

His face was bathed in sweat as he pushed himself backward a few inches. Exploring with his hands, he found the place where the tunnel grew smaller. His fingers dug into the rotten wood and tore pieces of it away. Worms were burrowing there, and his fingers grew slick with the juices of the ones he crushed. At the moment, he didn't care. If some worm guts helped him ease his way through the narrow passage, then he was glad for the sacrifice they were making in his behalf.

He pushed forward again. For a second he thought his shoulders were going to stick again, but then they slipped through. His hips were smaller, and they cleared the bottleneck easily.

"Shit! I can't figure this out. You sure he didn't get past you, Durkin?"

"Damn right he didn't get past me! What do you take me for, Avery, a fool?"

"Keep your suspenders on! Hell, I didn't mean no offense. It's just that I know the boss wanted this badge-totin' sidewinder dead, and we were supposed to go along when the rest of the boys hit that lumber camp too."

"We'll be done here in plenty of time for the raid. I know that jasper was wounded—I saw the blood on his shirt when he fell off his horse. He can't have gotten very far. We just have to find him."

The words "raid" and "lumber camp" echoed in Longarm's head with a sound just as hollow as this tree he was crawling through. Whoever these bushwhackers were, no matter what the identity of the mysterious boss they worked for, one thing was crystal clear to Longarm.

There was going to be an attack on the McEntire lumber camp—and that would likely mean that Aurora's life would be in danger.

Now more than ever, it was vitally important for him to get out of there. He wasn't sure when the raid was planned, but the men he had heard talking had sounded as if it wasn't too far off. He had to get away from these men and make it to the camp so that he could warn Aurora of the impending attack.

Suddenly, there was a thump behind him. Someone had struck the log with a gun butt, or a clenched fist, or something. What it was didn't really matter. What was important was the echo that resounded from inside the fallen tree.

Longarm pushed himself harder, faster. The seconds were slipping away. . . .

"Hey! This tree's hollow. You don't think—"

"Son of a bitch! He's inside the tree!"

Time was up.

Chapter 8

Longarm wasn't far from the end of the tree now, and this was where the disease had been the worst, where the wood was the most rotten. He pushed himself onto hands and knees, arching his injured back against the trunk. Pain washed through him, a red-tinged agony that might have made him pass out had his effort not been fueled by desperation. With a splintering sound that he hoped was from the tree, he emerged with pieces of rotten wood showering around him.

Dizzy from the pain, he threw himself to the side as guns began to bang. The shots came from the other end of the tree, however, where he had crawled into it. He twisted, catching his balance, and yanked his Colt from the cross-draw rig. Firing as much from instinct as anything else, he snapped a couple of shots toward the bushwhackers, and was rewarded by the sight of one of the men doubling over and collapsing. Longarm stumbled toward the trees.

The edge of the pine forest was only a few feet away here, and in a matter of seconds, Longarm was among the towering trees. He careened along in a staggering run, hoping that he wouldn't run into one of the pines and dash his brains out on its trunk. Shots still rang out behind him, but now they sounded slightly muffled. He didn't know if that was because the thick growth deadened the reports, or because his hearing was going. Either way, he had to keep moving.

Suddenly, his feet went out from under him. With a bone-jarring thump, he sat down hard and started sliding. Realizing that he had fallen into a gully, he reached out blindly in an effort to grab something and slow down his slide.

His fingers hooked around the base of a bush. He closed them tightly, and as the bush's roots held, Longarm came to an abrupt halt. He lay there on the steep slope and looked around, blinking sweat out of his eyes. The gully was a deep one, about forty feet, and he had slid about halfway down the side of it. At the bottom of the gully, a small creek bubbled along over a narrow, rocky bed. The noise it made sounded loud to Longarm, but not so loud that he could not hear the voices shouting in the woods above him.

"He headed over this way! I heard him!"

"Be careful, damn it! He may be trying to set up an ambush."

"Ambush, hell! The bastard was half dead when he busted out of that hollow log. I saw him, and he could barely move."

A third voice said, "He moved well enough to kill Durkin."

Longarm felt a little tingle of satisfaction at the knowledge that he had downed one of the bushwhackers. Evidently there were three of them left, however, and they were in the process of hunting him down. If he stayed here, it probably wouldn't take them very long to find him, and he'd be an easy target perched here on the side of the gully like this.

Time to get moving again, he told himself grimly.

Now that he wasn't sliding out of control, he was able to slip down the side of the gully without crashing through the brush. After a moment, he reached the little stream, and he went to one knee beside it to scoop up some water and splash it in his face and over his head. Fed by snowmelt from the peaks of the Cascades, the water was icy cold and made Longarm gasp and shiver. It drove back some of the mental cobwebs that threatened to overwhelm him, however, and that was what he wanted. He cupped more of the water in his free hand and sucked it down thirstily.

Longarm pushed himself back to his feet. The creek was so narrow that he was able to step over it, even in his weakened condition. The slope on the other side of the gully was not as steep. He angled along it, gradually working his way upward, using the trees and brush that dotted the ground as cover. He heard the searchers moving around on the other side of the creek and stepped up his pace.

Catching a glimpse of movement from the corner of his eye, Longarm knelt behind a clump of underbrush and went motionless. His eyes followed a flash of color that he spotted on the other side of the gully, and after a moment one of the bushwhackers stepped into clear view. Longarm had had only a very fleeting look at them when he burst free of the log and traded shots with them before dashing into the forest. Now he saw that this man wore range clothes, including a high-crowned hat and a cowhide vest. Like the man who had opened fire on Longarm and Wing when they were on their way back to the Diamond K from Timber City, this gent was dressed like a cowboy. And also like that other fella, this one was a complete stranger to Longarm too.

The clothes didn't have to mean anything. Owlhoots, hired guns, were generally much more likely to dress like cowboys than like lumberjacks. These men could have been hired by Ben Callahan or even Aurora herself, though Longarm had come to the conclusion that his suspicions about her were unfounded. Aurora wouldn't hire gunmen to raid her own camp. That wouldn't accomplish a damned thing.

Callahan was a different story. If he was bound and determined to make things so difficult for Aurora that she would have no choice except to sell her company to him, then an attack by these cowboys and other hired guns like them might do the trick.

Personally, Longarm thought, Callahan—or whoever the boss was—had underestimated Aurora. She was a proud, stubborn woman. He knew that just by the way she had made the timber company she had inherited from her late husband into even more of a success.

But all the pondering in the world wouldn't mean a damn thing, Longarm reminded himself, unless he got away from these killers and made it to the timber camp in time to warn Aurora of the attack. He stayed absolutely still, watching the bushwhacker on the other side of the gully through a tiny gap in the screen of brush.

The man poked around a little, started trying to make his way down the slope, then changed his mind and pulled himself back up to the edge of the gully. Like Longarm, he had a gun fisted in one hand. Only about thirty feet separated the two of them, and Longarm was worried that his breathing would give him away. Despite his best efforts, the pain of his wound lent a harshness to every breath he drew. Evidently, though, the chuckling of the creek was enough to cover up the slight noises.

Longarm learned suddenly that he was wrong. Either that or the fella had spotted him somehow, because the gunman abruptly whirled toward him, jerked up the pistol, and yelled, "He's over here!" as he squeezed the trigger.

Longarm threw himself to the side, catching hold of the brush with one hand to steady himself as the bushwhacker's bullet ripped through the leaves about a foot away. Fighting off the blurriness that tried to take over his vision, Longarm fired twice. The first slug chewed bark off the trunk of a pine right behind the gunman, but the second bored into the man's chest and threw him back against the tree. The gunman bounced off the trunk, tried to stay upright, and failed. As the gun slipped from his fingers, he pitched forward, falling into the gully and tumbling head over heels down the slope until he came to a stop with his upper body in the creek at the bottom. He lay motionless, tendrils of red seeping into the water as it flowed around him.

That was two of them accounted for, Longarm realized as he pushed himself to his feet. This was no time to congratulate himself, though. Instead he turned and started for the top of the slope as fast as he could force himself to move, no longer worrying about any noise he might make. The bushwhacker's yell and the exchange of shots would bring the other two killers on the run.

Shots banged behind him. He heard the whisper of bullets through the leaves and the thud of slugs hitting tree trunks. Then he was at the top, powering over and throwing himself once more into the shelter of the thick forest.

In his pain-wracked state, it seemed like hours, even days, had passed since the initial volley of shots that had knocked him out of the roan's saddle. Surely he had been playing cat and mouse through these woods with the killers for at least that long. But his brain told him that no more than twenty minutes, half an hour at the most, had passed. He still had time to alert the McEntire camp to the raid if he could get away from the remaining two gunmen.

And find his way out of the forest. That might not be easy, given the shape he was in. Normally he had an extremely good sense of direction, which had served to save his life on more than one occasion in the past. That might not be the case today.

He ran blindly, darting this way, angling off in another direction, zigzagging yet another way. He might even be running in circles for all he knew. Distantly, he heard the men coming after him. Occasionally, a shot resounded through the forest as one of them blazed away at something they thought was him, but as far as Longarm could tell, none of the bullets came anywhere close to him.

Unfortunately, his strength was deserting him. His run had turned into a stagger, and he had to keep clutching at tree trunks to keep from falling flat on his face. Once again, time was running out on him.

He stumbled forward, and it took him a moment to realize that he had emerged from the trees once more.

Longarm stopped short, shaking his head and looking around. He *had* been running in circles, because he was back on the trail. Not only that, but when he heard a surprised whinny, he looked up and saw the roan about fifty feet away. The horse had been calmly grazing on the grass at the side of the trail when Longarm came floundering out of the woods.

Longarm held out a hand and called softly to the roan. He started toward the animal, and it nervously backed away from him a few steps. Longarm couldn't blame the horse. Covered with blood and smeared with filth from the inside of the log, he probably looked bad and smelled worse. But the roan was his one chance to get out of this mess and maybe salvage something from it, so he wasn't going to let the horse get away.

One foot in front of the other, Longarm told himself. Steady, slow and steady. He kept talking, nonsense intended only to soothe the horse's jitters. It must have worked, because the roan stopped backing away. In fact, it even came forward a few steps and nuzzled curiously against his outstretched hand.

Longarm caught hold of the dangling reins and moved to the horse's left side. As he reached up to grasp the saddle horn, he wondered how the roan had gotten so tall. Pulling himself all the way up into the saddle seemed like an almost insurmountable task. With a groan of effort, Longarm got a foot in the stirrup and then hauled himself up. He settled down in the saddle with a thump that made fresh waves of pain ripple through his wounded back.

He slumped forward and jammed his heels into the roan's flanks. The horse broke into a trot. Longarm gritted his teeth and hissed, "Son of a bitch!" through tightly clenched jaws. Every step the roan took hurt him like blazes.

He was moving, though, and that was the important thing. Longarm lifted his head and peered around, trying to orient himself. He had been on the trail to the Diamond K when he was ambushed, and that was still where he was, he realized as he noted several landmarks. More importantly, he was headed back toward the main trail, the one that would ultimately take him to the McEntire Timber Company camp.

Shouts ripped through the stillness of the forest behind him, followed an instant later by the crash of gunshots. Longarm twisted in the saddle, hanging on tightly with one hand while he used the other to empty his pistol toward the surviving bushwhackers, who had also reached the trail. He didn't know if he hit either of them or not, but he didn't feel the impact of any fresh lead. That was all he cared about at the moment. "Run, damn it, run!" he called to the roan as he drove his heels once more into its flanks.

The bushwhackers were on foot, and they would have to find their horses again before they could come after him. That would give him enough of a lead, Longarm realized, that they would never catch up to him.

Of course, he had been convinced of things before and then had them backfire on him, so it wouldn't do to get over-confident. He kept the roan moving at a steady run until he reached the main trail.

Longarm reined in and paused to study the landscape, trying to remember which way he was supposed to turn. Instinct told him to turn right, toward the south, but for some reason his brain insisted that he go north. He scowled as he tried to puzzle it out.

His gut feelings had saved his life in the past—but so had his mental processes. At the moment, however, he put more stock in his instincts, since his head was more than a little addled. He swung the roan's head to the right and urged it into a run again.

Afterwards, Longarm didn't remember much of that ride. He realized he must have been slipping in and out of consciousness. But he was in one of his lucid moments when he reached the cutoff to the logging camp, and he swung the horse onto the smaller trail with scarcely a reduction in speed.

He expected to be stopped by one of the sentries, as usual, but no one stepped out of the trees to challenge him. Somewhere in the back of his mind, Longarm knew that wasn't a good sign. He pushed on, the fear that he might be too late clearing his head somewhat.

As he drew closer to the camp, that worry intensified. The guard shack was deserted. He slowed the horse's mad dash for a moment, expecting to hear gunfire up ahead. But silence was the only thing that greeted him. When he rounded a turn in the trail and passed through an open spot in the canopy of trees, he saw smoke curling into the sky, rising from a spot higher on the mountain.

A spot just about where the McEntire camp was located.

Longarm yelled at the roan and banged his heels into its sides, urging more speed from the horse. The roan responded, lunging forward into a gallop. Longarm had moved beyond pain now; his injured back was numb, and he didn't feel the pounding of the roan's increased speed.

Sweeping wide around bends in the trail, the horse ran flat out for several minutes before the timber camp came into view. As Longarm had feared, that was the source of the smoke. Dark billows rose from the long barracks-like building where the loggers slept. The structure was being consumed by flames.

The fire wasn't the worst of it. Several men were sprawled around the clearing where the camp was located. Longarm had seen enough corpses in his life to know immediately that they were dead. Their bright-colored shirts were stained a dark red with blood.

The sawmill and Aurora's new cabin appeared to be undamaged, as was the cookshack. A line of men stretched from the creek beside the sawmill to the burning barracks, passing buckets back and forth as they battled the blaze. The efforts of the bucket brigade weren't going to be enough, Longarm saw as he reined the horse to a halt. The fire was too far advanced already. Wetting down the area around the building might keep the flames from spreading, however, and that appeared to be what the loggers turned their attention to as Longarm watched.

He was close enough to feel heat from the flames pushing against his face. Despite that, a cold chill went through him. Nothing was more deadly, or more feared, in the woods than fire. Luckily, the season had been a fairly wet one, and the trees were green and healthy. Still, once a forest fire got going, it was almost impossible to put out.

Longarm pushed that thought from his mind. The loggers were doing everything they could to contain the fire. Right now, finding out what had happened to Aurora McEntire was of more compelling urgency to Longarm.

He looked around the camp as he dismounted awkwardly, his normally smooth motions hampered by the injury he had suffered. He held on to the reins for support and led the horse toward Aurora's cabin.

She emerged from the door before he got there, trailed by Jared Flint. Aurora had her head turned and was giving orders to her harried-looking foreman, so she didn't see Longarm right away. That gave him a chance to look at her and assure himself that she was really all right. Her hair and clothing were disheveled, and there was a smudge of something, either ashes or blood, on her cheek, but other than that, she appeared to be unharmed. Longarm lifted a hand and called, "Mrs. McEntire!"

She turned quickly toward him and gasped when she saw the blood and dirt covering him. "Marshal Long!" she exclaimed as she rushed over to him. "What happened to you?"

"Ran into some fellas who . . . tried to kill me," Longarm said wearily. "I disabused 'em of that notion."

Aurora took hold of his arm, her touch soft yet firm at the same time. "Come inside," she urged him. "We have some other wounded men in the cabin, and I'm doing what I can for them." Her attitude was brisk and businesslike, but Longarm could see shining in her eyes a concern for him that had no doubt grown out of their passionate encounter earlier in the day.

"I'll keep that bucket brigade going," said Flint as he started toward the burning building. He echoed Longarm's concern by adding, "We've got to stop that fire before it reaches the trees."

"Amen to that," muttered Aurora as she gently tugged Longarm toward the cabin.

"Tried to . . . get here and warn you," Longarm told her. "Sorry I wasn't . . . in time."

She paused and looked at him in surprise. "You knew this was going to happen?"

"Heard the gents who . . . bushwhacked me . . . talking about it. Didn't think it was supposed to happen . . . this soon."

"They struck quickly," Aurora said. "There was no warning. No one was in camp except the men working in the mill and myself." She helped him step into the cabin. One man, probably the most badly wounded of the lot, was lying in the bed Aurora and Longarm had put to such good use, while half a dozen more injured men had been made comfortable on pallets laid out on the floor. "Those cowboys rode in whooping and shooting," Aurora went on, "and when the men in the mill ran out to see what was happening, the raiders just shot them down in cold blood."

Longarm felt a fierce anger welling up inside him. He experienced the same thing every time he encountered violence and murder and all the things that went with one bunch of people thinking they could run roughshod over another bunch. The rage he felt was not enough to counteract the weariness and loss of blood, however, and he felt himself beginning to sag.

"Best get me . . . into that chair over by the table," he said to Aurora.

She had an arm around his waist now, being careful not to touch his back. Carefully, she helped him sit down straddling the chair. Then she reached for a knife that was lying on the table. "I'm going to cut that shirt off of you," she said. "Then we'll have a look at what happened to you."

"Best tend to . . . these other fellas," said Longarm.

Aurora shook her head. "I've already done everything I can for them. Mr. Flint sent a rider to Timber City to fetch a doctor."

Longarm nodded. Aurora's deft hands were using the knife to slice through his bloody shirt and lay it back to expose the wound. He heard her catch her breath. It had to be ugly.

"What happened?"

"Bullet creased me. Bastards were waiting for me. I think the slug . . . clipped my left shoulder blade . . . too. But it didn't do worse than . . . chip it a little." He rotated his left arm and shoulder, wincing as he did so. "I can still use this wing, so I reckon there's no real damage."

"Sit still. I'll clean this up."

She stepped away from him for a moment, then returned. He was surprised when she came around the chair and lifted a bottle of whiskey to his mouth. "Better swallow some of this," she said as she tilted the bottle. "It won't hurt as much outside if you've got a healthy swallow of it inside."

That was a reasonable attitude, Longarm decided, so he took a long drink of the whiskey. Then Aurora went behind him and doused the stuff on the bullet crease that he had torn up even worse by crawling through the log, and he had to bite his lip to keep from howling in pain. After a moment the burning subsided, and Longarm closed his eyes in relief.

That didn't last long. Aurora began dabbing at the wound with a cloth soaked in whiskey, and the fiery pain came back. Longarm withstood it stoically.

To distract himself, he thought about the attack on the camp. The way those bushwhackers had been talking, the raid had been planned for later in the day. Despite his befuddled state, surely it hadn't taken him *that* long to reach the camp. No, the boss must have speeded up the schedule for some reason, Longarm decided. Maybe when the bushwhackers hadn't returned right away to report that Longarm was dead, their unknown leader had figured that he couldn't take a chance on the big lawman turning into a wild card that might ruin the play. It was a feasible theory, thought Longarm.

"The doctor may want to sew this up when he gets here," said Aurora.

Longarm shook his head. Something was eating at him, something he had seen outside that was wrong, and as he sat there at the table, he finally figured out what it was. The loggers working higher on the mountain should have heard the gunfire, and they certainly would have seen the smoke. Yet there had been only a relative handful of men fighting the fire outside, and those were probably some of the sawmill workers.

He twisted his head to look up at Aurora. "Where . . . where are the rest of your men?"

Her lovely face was set in lines of hatred now. "They've gone to put a stop to this once and for all. They're headed for the Diamond K, and when they get there, they're going to burn it to the ground—just like Kinsman's men tried to do to us."

Chapter 9

Longarm would have surged up out of the chair had it not been for Aurora's hand on his shoulder pressing him down. "Damn it!" he exclaimed. "They can't do that!"

"Why not?" asked Aurora, her voice a little chilly now. "Surely after this you can't keep on making excuses for Kinsman, Marshal."

Longarm glared up at her. "I'm not making excuses for anybody," he said. "I just don't want innocent folks getting killed."

"There's no one innocent on the Diamond K."

Longarm thought about Molly and Wing and felt a fresh surge of anger at Aurora's attitude. She wouldn't understand that, though, not in her current frame of mind, so he said, "What about your men? You don't think Kinsman and his riders will just let them waltz in there and set fire to the place, do you? I'll tell you what's going to happen. Kinsman will fight back, and a lot of men will wind up dying—on both sides."

A look of concern appeared on Aurora's face. "Maybe

you're right,'' she said grudgingly. "But there was no way I could stop them. Several men were killed in the raid, and the rest of them were out to avenge their friends.''

Longarm reached for the bottle of whiskey, which Aurora had placed on the table after soaking the cloth she had used to clean his wound. He took another slug of the fiery stuff, then wiped the back of his other hand across his mouth. "Tear up a petticoat or something and wrap the strips around me to bind up that crease,'' he said curtly. "Then I want to borrow a shirt if you've got one.''

"I can find something for you to wear . . . but you're not going anywhere, Marshal. Not until the doctor's taken a look at you.''

"The hell I'm not,'' growled Longarm. "I've got to put a stop to this if I can.'' The anger he felt—and the restorative jolt of the whiskey, to be honest—had given him back some of his strength, buoyed him to the point that he thought he could ride again.

"Surely you don't actually think Kinsman is innocent,'' Aurora said in a mixture of amazement and indignation.

"I haven't seen a lick of proof that he's guilty,'' Longarm shot back. "I got a pretty good look at one of the gents who ambushed me today, and he wasn't one of Kinsman's riders. Neither was the man who tried to kill me yesterday. Somebody's spooked, Aurora, and is trying to get me out of the way.''

He still liked Ben Callahan for that role. Admittedly, he couldn't be sure that Callahan even knew of his existence, let alone that he was a deputy U.S. marshal, but it was possible, especially if, as Longarm suspected, Callahan had at least one man here in the McEntire camp who was really on his payroll. Longarm's true identity was common knowledge among the loggers, and if Callahan had an inside man, the information could have been passed along easily to the rival timber company owner.

"Regardless of whether what you say is true or not, you're not going anywhere.'' Aurora shook her head stubbornly. "You're in no shape to ride.''

"The hell with it," Longarm muttered. Roughly, he shook off her hand and stood up. "I'll go like this."

Aurora looked shocked at his vehemence. "Wait a minute," she said quickly. "If you're that determined . . ."

"We're wasting time," Longarm said grimly.

"I'll do what you asked." Hurriedly, Aurora tore an undergarment into strips to bind up Longarm's wound, then produced a man's shirt from a trunk. "It was one of Angus's," she said. "The sleeves may be a little short."

They were, but Longarm didn't care. Whatever he was going to do, he had to do it before he lost his second wind.

Because once that was gone, he likely wouldn't be able to do anything for a while except collapse.

He left the cabin as he was shrugging into the shirt and fastening a couple of its buttons. While he looked around for the roan, he thumbed fresh cartridges into the Colt, then holstered it. The horse was nearby, standing where Longarm had dropped its reins.

Aurora had followed him out of the cabin. "I'm coming with you," she said.

Longarm looked at her in surprise. "You can't do that."

"The hell I can't, as you would say. I can be every bit as stubborn as you, Marshal."

Longarm had already figured that out about her, and even as he drew a breath to argue, he knew it would be useless. So he said instead, "All right. But if there's trouble, you stay out of the way."

She made no reply, just headed for a small corral near the cookshack where several saddle horses were kept.

The fire in the barracks was burning itself out following the collapse of the structure, and the flames didn't seem to have spread, as Longarm saw to his considerable relief. Jared Flint turned away from the ashes of the building and then started quickly toward Longarm and Aurora, his brow creasing in surprise and concern above his bushy eyebrows. "Miz McEntire," he said as Aurora led a horse from the corral, "what are you doing, ma'am?"

"I'm going with Marshal Long," Aurora told him. "Will you saddle this horse for me, Mr. Flint?"

"Sure, but—are you certain that's a good idea?" Flint inclined his head toward Longarm. "No offense to the marshal, but he looks pretty banged up."

"He is," said Aurora, "but we're going to do what we can to stop the men from attacking the Diamond K. Marshal Long is worried—and I share his concern—that some of our men may be killed when they confront Kinsman and his blood-thirsty cowboys."

She just couldn't resist doing a little editorializing, thought Longarm. But overall, he was glad she had decided to come with him. If they reached Kinsman's ranch in time to stop the loggers from attacking, the men would be more likely to obey Aurora's orders than his. If she told them to give up their thoughts of revenge, they might go along with her wishes.

Of course, it might already be too late, and that thought gnawed at Longarm's gut. Just as he had worried that some harm might come to Aurora in the attack on the camp, now he was concerned about the safety of Molly Kinsman, not to mention the others on the ranch for whom he had felt an instinctive liking, such as Wing and Joe Traywick.

Not surprisingly, Jared Flint saddled a horse for himself as well as one for Aurora. When she saw that her foreman intended to go along, Aurora's mouth tightened, but she didn't say anything. Together with Longarm, they rode out of the camp, Flint taking the lead. Instead of following the usual trail, however, Flint took a smaller path that curved over the shoulder of the mountain.

"This is the way the boys went," he said. "It's a little closer to the Diamond K this way than it is going all the way back to the main trail."

So that explained why he hadn't run into the rampaging lumberjacks on his way to the camp, thought Longarm. They had taken a different route.

Even so, it seemed to take a long time to reach Matt Kinsman's ranch. Longarm rapidly became lost as the trail twisted and turned through the woods. After a while, Aurora grew concerned too, and asked Flint, "Shouldn't we be getting there by now?"

Before Flint could answer, the sound of distant gunfire came to their ears.

Longarm bit back a curse, knowing that what he was hearing signaled the beginning of the battle between the loggers and the cowboys of the Diamond K. Grimly, Flint said, "Sounds like we're too late."

"Maybe not," Longarm grated. "Maybe we can stop it before too many men get ventilated." He prodded the roan forward, not looking back to see if Aurora and Flint were following. The horse was getting tired—but then so was Longarm. The reserves of strength he had replenished earlier were running out again.

Guided by the gunfire, Longarm made his way through the pines. They grew closely together in places, so that he had to thread his way among them. Aurora and Flint had to ride single file behind him much of the time. The shooting grew steadily louder, and finally Longarm emerged on a long ridge that was more sparsely wooded than the slopes behind him. The ground fell away in front of him to the valley where the headquarters of the Diamond K were located.

Down below, the loggers from the McEntire camp were advancing on the ranch, using trees and brush and rocks for cover as they fired Winchesters toward the cluster of buildings. There weren't enough rifles to go around, so the men who didn't have guns were armed with the double-bitted axes they used in their work. Those deadly tools could fell a tree in a matter of minutes in the skillful hands of their owners. In close fighting, they could chop down a human being even faster.

A heavy return fire came from the ranch buildings. Longarm scanned the slope below him, expecting to see that some of the lumberjacks had already fallen. They had been lucky, though; all of them were still on their feet.

That situation wouldn't stay the same. Sooner or later, some of the bullets flying around down there would find their targets in soft flesh.

And those in the ranch buildings were in danger too. Longarm could just imagine Molly Kinsman crouched near one of the windows in the house, reloading for her father and Joe Traywick. Either that, or she might even be wielding a rifle

101

herself. A stray slug could find her just as easily as anyone else.

Longarm pulled his Colt and aimed into the air. He squeezed off three shots, then bellowed, "Hold your fire, damn it! McEntire men, hold your fire!"

As he expected, they pretty much ignored him, except for quick glances that several of them threw over their shoulders before they went back to fighting.

They didn't ignore Aurora, though. She burst past Longarm, gigging her horse into a breakneck run that carried her down the ridge toward her employees. Longarm yelled, "Wait—" but he was too late. As Aurora dashed downward into danger, Longarm said bitterly, fervently, "Hell!"

"Stop it! Stop shooting!" Aurora's voice rang out clear and strong, and even over the clamor of battle, some of the men heard it. The ones who did turned and looked in amazement at her, galloping down the slope at such a pace that it seemed her horse was in imminent danger of falling and pitching her off. Somehow she stayed upright as she shouted for the loggers to put an end to the fight.

Longarm and Flint were right behind her, struggling to keep up. Longarm hoped none of the ranch's defenders saw them and thought they were reinforcements for the attacking lumberjacks. Aurora's dark hair had come loose from its usual bun, and Longarm was glad of that. Streaming out behind her as she rode, Aurora's hair immediately marked her as a woman. Longarm kept one hand on the reins and began waving the other over his head, hoping that those in the buildings below would see him and realize he was trying to get them to hold their fire.

The loggers' rifles gradually fell silent, and so too did those of the Diamond K. Longarm spotted several men scurrying around the ranch buildings, no doubt spreading the word that a momentary cease-fire had been called. What he had to do now was insure that the cessation of hostilities was permanent, not temporary.

He rode up next to Aurora and said in a low voice, "That was a damn fool stunt."

"It got them to stop shooting, didn't it?" she replied with a defiant toss of her head.

Longarm had to admit she was right about that. He looked along the line of men who had been attacking the ranch. Now that he was closer, he could see that they had not gone completely unscathed so far. One man's left arm hung limp from a bullet that had bored through it, while several others sported bloodstains on their clothes from creases much like the one on Longarm's back. Such wounds were messy but seldom fatal. Didn't stop them from hurting like blazes, though.

Longarm noticed as well that even though the guns had fallen silent, the loggers weren't emerging from their cover. The battle could start again in a matter of seconds if things didn't go well.

Jared Flint rode up beside Longarm and Aurora and said ominously, "I don't trust those cowboys down there, Miz McEntire. If they start shooting again, you're right out in the open."

"Maybe that will be reason enough to keep them from firing," said Aurora. She looked over at Longarm. "I'm going down there, Marshal."

"Well, then, I'm going with you," said Longarm.

"I figured you would. Your little masquerade as a cowboy may be over."

Longarm shrugged. "I never expected it to last very long anyway, and it wasn't paying any dividends."

Aurora glanced at her foreman. "Mr. Flint, I expect you to keep the men in line. There'll be no trouble, no shooting."

Flint glowered a little, but after a moment he nodded and said, "Yes, ma'am. No trouble—as long as you're down there."

Longarm and Aurora rode slowly, side by side, down the hill toward the ranch. All movement had ceased around the buildings, Longarm noticed. Kinsman and his men were hunkering down and waiting to see what was going to happen too, just like the lumberjacks.

Matt Kinsman and Joe Traywick emerged onto the porch of the big house as Longarm and Aurora drew rein in front of it. Longarm tried to look past them for any sign of Molly, but he didn't see her. All he could do was hope that she was somewhere in the house, unharmed by the bullets that had been flying a few minutes earlier.

"Custis!" exclaimed Kinsman as he realized who was accompanying Aurora. "What are you doing with that . . . that Jezebel?"

"Well, now, we're going to have to talk about that, Mr. Kinsman," said Longarm. "Is it all right if Mrs. McEntire and I light and set for a spell?"

"I'm a hospitable man," Kinsman said with a glower, "but I'll be damned if I let that woman in my house!"

Aurora said coolly, "I feel the same way, Mr. Kinsman, so I'll say what I have to say out here. Can I count on your men to honor the truce?"

"I don't see no white flag, Boss," Traywick put in. Like Kinsman, he held a Winchester in his hands and seemed ready to use it.

"That don't make no difference, Joe," Kinsman said. Then he turned to Aurora. "As long as those men of yours don't start shootin', neither will we. Now, if you've got somethin' to say, woman, spit it out."

Longarm glanced over at Aurora, hoping she could keep a tight rein on her temper. With a visible effort, she did so. "What I want to know, Mr. Kinsman, is why your cowboys raided my camp earlier this afternoon and killed some of my men."

Kinsman pulled his head back and squinted at her as if she had just slapped him in the face. "Hellfire and damnation!" he exploded after a moment. "What in blazes are you talkin' about?"

"I think you know," Aurora said tautly.

Longarm was watching Kinsman closely, and he was convinced that the rancher *didn't* have the slightest idea what Aurora was talking about. The accusation had come as a complete surprise to him. Beside him, Joe Traywick looked just as shocked and baffled.

"None of my men have been off the ranch today," Kinsman insisted, " 'cept for Custis there." He waved a hand at Longarm, then narrowed his eyes suspiciously at the lawman.

"And you still ain't explained what's goin' on, son."

Longarm didn't see any good way out of this, other than telling the truth. He said, "Custis is just the first part of my handle, Mr. Kinsman. The other part is Long. I'm a deputy United States marshal working out of the Denver office. My boss sent me up here because the trouble between you and Mrs. McEntire is jeopardizing a government lumber contract."

For a moment, Kinsman stared at Longarm in amazement; then his flushed face turned an even darker shade of red as anger surged up inside him. "You lied to me!" he accused.

"More like I just . . . left out a few things." Longarm went on quickly. "And that ain't really important now. What matters is that Mrs. McEntire is telling the truth about the raid on her camp. A handful of men are dead and a building's been burned down. There are plenty of witnesses to say that the men who did the killing and burning were dressed like cowboys."

"That don't make 'em cowboys," snapped Kinsman, "and it sure as hell don't make 'em Diamond K hands."

"Could it have been some of your boys, not acting on orders, just doing something they figured you'd approve of?"

Instead of answering Longarm's question directly, Kinsman turned to Traywick. "You know the whereabouts of all the hands, Joe?"

"Of course I do," replied Traywick with a snort of disgust. "They're all on Diamond K's home range. I'd stake my life on it."

Kinsman turned back toward Longarm and Aurora with a look of smug satisfaction on his florid face. "Looks to me like the only attack around here was the one your men just launched on my ranch, ma'am. And it was mighty unprovoked, if you ask me."

"That's your story?" Aurora asked coldly.

"And I'm stickin' to it."

"Then who raided my camp?"

Traywick said, "Just 'cause some gents have range duds on don't make 'em real cowboys." He snorted again and waved toward the ridge overlooking the ranch headquarters. "Hell, you could dress up those lumberjacks of yours, and *they* might look like cowboys!''

That same thought had already occurred to Longarm. The raiders could have been loggers from Ben Callahan's camp, disguised as cowhands to shift the blame onto the Diamond K. If that was the case, the ruse had been a stunning success, at least at first.

As Aurora considered what Kinsman and Traywick had said, Longarm thought he saw something like doubt appear in her eyes for the first time. That was a step in the right direction, he thought. If he could get both Aurora and Kinsman to admit that someone else might be to blame for their problems, he would have a better chance of getting to the bottom of this. His investigation was bound to go more smoothly without having to worry all the time about the loggers and the Diamond K hands trying to kill each other.

''Well,'' said Kinsman, ''what're we goin' to do about this? I don't trust Miz McEntire, and I don't much reckon she trusts me.''

''You're right about that,'' said Aurora.

Kinsman turned a baleful stare on Longarm. ''And I ain't overly fond of what you did, Marshal.''

''Just trying to do my job,'' said Longarm. ''And as for what the two of you are going to do, I figure the best thing would be to make this truce permanent. Have your men steer clear of that lumber camp, Mr. Kinsman. You tell your men to do likewise where the Diamond K is concerned, ma'am. That way, if there's any more trouble, you'll know for sure that neither of you is to blame.''

''Well . . .'' Kinsman said grudgingly, ''I reckon that might work.''

''It means we'd have to trust each other,'' Aurora pointed out.

''Or try to anyway,'' Longarm said.

Kinsman nodded abruptly. ''I'll do it, leastways for the time bein'.''

''My men won't like it,'' said Aurora, ''but I'll make them listen to reason.''

Longarm felt a surge of relief. With both Kinsman and Aurora being reasonable about things, he had a chance to actually do some good and find out who was really behind the killings and the other trouble in these parts. Whether it was Ben Callahan or someone else entirely, Longarm intended to bring whoever had hired those owlhoots to justice.

Along with the relief came a wave of weariness. It had been a damned hard day, and it was difficult for him to believe that only this morning he had appeared before that coroner's jury in Timber City. Since then he had bedded Aurora McEntire, been ambushed and wounded by the men working for that mysterious boss, fought his way out of that trouble, reached the lumber camp too late to prevent more murders, and raced here to the Diamond K in a desperate attempt to forestall an even more wholesale slaughter. Along the way he'd lost a heap of blood and endured more pain than any man ought to be expected to endure.

Yep, that was a full day's work, all right, he thought.

That was almost the last thing that went through his mind before blackness reached out unexpectedly to claim him. He felt himself swaying in the saddle and reached for the saddlehorn, knowing that he was about to fall. His fingers clutched at the horn but slipped off it. As he tumbled off the roan, he vaguely heard a voice—no, two voices, *female* voices, cry out, "Custis!"

One of the voices belonged to Aurora, the other to Molly Kinsman. Aurora and Molly . . . that might prove to be interesting.

Too bad he wasn't going to be awake to see what happened.

That was his last thought as he slipped away into nothingness.

Chapter 10

Longarm woke to a soft, cool touch on his brow. *Angels?* he thought. Not likely. Not after the life he'd led. A fella with a tail and a pitchfork would be more like it.

But wherever he was now, it wasn't hot, and instead of brimstone, he smelled the clean fragrance of a woman's hair. More of his senses began to return to him, and he realized he was lying on his belly on soft sheets with his face turned to the side so that it wouldn't be buried in the pillow underneath his head. A sheet covered his lower half.

He was stark naked too. That discovery made Longarm open his eyes to see what the hell was going on.

"You're awake. Good. I was worried about you, Custis."

It was Molly Kinsman's voice, hovering somewhere closely above him. With a grunt of effort, wincing from sore muscles, Longarm pushed himself up slightly so that he could look around. Molly was sitting on the edge of the bed beside him, and he could see genuine concern in her green eyes. He saw something else too . . . anger maybe.

"What . . ." he managed to say.

"You're in the spare bedroom in the ranch house," she told him. "I figure where you are is what a man like you would want to know first. A U.S. marshal."

Yep, she was definitely mad at him, he thought. Her voice had dripped scorn when she mentioned his real identity.

"Deputy U.S. marshal," he corrected her. "My boss is the chief marshal in the Denver office."

Molly stood up, making the bed's mattress bounce a little. Longarm's injured back twinged.

"What does it matter?" she demanded. "You still lied to me, lied to all of us. The only reason you came here is to spy on us!"

Longarm propped himself on his elbows and regarded her solemnly. "I got the impression a few minutes ago, Molly, that you were worried about me."

"I was," she snapped. Her voice softened a little as she went on. "When I saw you fall off your horse outside, and when I saw the bloodstains on your back, I knew you'd been hurt bad." She drew a deep breath. "But that was before I thought about who you really are and why you came to the Diamond K! You're just here to protect that . . . that hussy!"

"You mean Aurora McEntire?"

"Of course that's who I mean! All you care about is that government timber contract I heard you talking about. I was right inside the parlor, watching through the window. I heard the whole thing."

Longarm looked her over. She was wearing a dress again, a simple dress of light gray cotton. It clung to her lithe young body. At the moment, however, Longarm was less interested in her coltish figure than he was in whether or not she had been hurt in the fighting before he got there. He didn't see any sign of bulky bandages under the dress.

"Are you all right?" he asked her. "I was afraid you might catch a bullet, the way they were flying around so."

Molly shook her head. "A couple of the hands were wounded slightly when those loggers attacked the ranch, but that was all. No one was killed—on either side." She sounded a mite disappointed as she added that last part, thought Longarm.

He breathed a sigh of relief. "Glad Mrs. McEntire and I were in time to stop that battle 'fore it was too late."

"*She's* the one you ought to arrest. We haven't done anything wrong since this whole thing started."

Longarm didn't remind her of the ruckus in Timber City the day she had arrived from the East. That brawl wasn't the only one that had broken out between the cowboys and the lumberjacks either.

Fistfights were one thing, though, and full-scale war was another. If the truce between the two factions didn't hold long enough for him to run the real rascals to ground, war was what they would have here in the Cascades.

He put that thought aside for the moment and asked, "What time is it? How long have I been in here?" A glance at the window had already told him that night had fallen.

"It's about eight o'clock," Molly told him. "It was around five when you passed out in the yard."

So he had been unconscious for three hours. And before that, the day had been too busy for him to grab anything to eat. Breakfast in the hotel dining room in Timber City had been over twelve hours earlier, so no wonder he was suddenly ravenously hungry. And thirsty too, he realized.

"You think I could get something to eat and drink? My stomach thinks my throat's been cut, and I'm so dry I'm spitting cotton."

"Of course." Molly started toward the door, but added over her shoulder, "I'm still not sure you deserve it, but no one can say the Diamond K is inhospitable."

Longarm didn't argue the point with her. He just sank back down on the pillow and waited for her to return.

It wasn't Molly who came into the room a few minutes later carrying a tray, however. Wing grinned at Longarm and said, "Mist' Custis feelee much better now, yes?"

"Ah, hell, Wing, it's me, remember? I know how you really talk."

"Oh, yeah. I forgot. Once you get into a habit . . ." Wing set the tray down on a bedside table. "I brought you some stew and some coffee. Think you can handle that much?"

"Damn right." Longarm sat up and twisted around, wrapping the sheet around him. His back was sore, but it didn't keep him from moving. His stomach clenched in anticipation as he smelled the stew. He reached for the tray, and Wing helped him get it situated in his lap.

"What happened to your back?" asked the cook. "I got those bandages off of you, and it looked like somebody tried to plow a furrow across there."

"That's what they did," said Longarm, "only they used a bullet instead of a plow. It's just a deep crease."

"Well, you'll have a scar there, that's for sure." Wing gestured at Longarm's bare torso, which was crisscrossed with dozens of other reminders of past wounds. "Of course, it'll have plenty of company."

Longarm shrugged and swallowed a mouthful of stew, then reached for the steaming cup of Arbuckle's. "I've been knocked around a mite," he admitted.

Wing picked up a straight-backed chair, reversed it, and straddled it. "Hear tell that you're a lawman."

"Deputy U.S. marshal," Longarm confirmed.

"And you're helping out that McEntire woman, the one with the timber contract."

Longarm shook his head and said, "You're jumping to the same conclusion as everybody else around here. I work for Uncle Sam, not Aurora McEntire. All I'm trying to do is get to the bottom of all the trouble that the Diamond K and the McEntire Timber Company have been blaming each other for."

"You don't think those lumberjacks rustled our stock and poisoned our well?" Wing asked with a frown.

"No, I don't," Longarm said bluntly. "And I don't think anybody from the Diamond K has been attacking that logging operation either. I reckon somebody else is behind all of it, for reasons of his own." He didn't say anything about his suspicions of Ben Callahan.

Wing's frown deepened as he thought about what Longarm had said. "Maybe you're on to something," he said slowly. "Loggers and cattlemen don't get along that well to start with. I don't reckon it'd take much for some outsider to prod a grudge into outright fightin'."

"That's what I'm thinking too. Kinsman doesn't really want to believe that, though, and neither does Aurora McEntire."

Wing chuckled. "That McEntire woman sure acts like she's slapped her brand on you, Custis. She was mad as a wet hen when Miss Molly insisted on bringing you in the house after you fell off your horse. Didn't do her any good, though. Once Miss Molly makes up her mind about something, that's the end of it."

Longarm knew what he meant. He had encountered Molly's stubbornness himself. But Aurora was equally stubborn, and he supposed they were all lucky a brand-new fight hadn't broken out over who was going to nurse him back to health.

That thought reminded him that although his back was still sore, it didn't hurt quite as much as he would have expected it to. When he commented on that, Wing looked pleased and said, "I put some salve on there. That's what's making it feel better."

"Some ancient Chinese remedy?"

Wing's grin widened. "How'd you guess?"

Longarm scraped the last of the soup out of the bowl and drained the coffee cup. He felt pretty much human again, just extremely tired. His weariness was growing by the moment, and he felt his eyelids beginning to droop. "You best take this tray, Wing," he said. "I'm feeling a mite puny again."

"Get some rest," Wing told him as he took the tray. "You'll feel better tomorrow."

Longarm lay on his side, being careful not to put any pressure on his injured back. Wing turned down the wick on the bedside lamp, leaving only a small flame burning, then slipped out of the room. Longarm heard the door closing softly behind the cook.

Eyes closed, Longarm waited for sleep. As he was drifting on the edge of awareness, something brushed at his brain, a feather-light touch that he knew was trying to alert him to something important.

But before he could grasp it, it slipped away, and so did he.

Longarm spent the next three days recuperating. Plenty of sleep, Wing's good cooking, and the salve that the cook daubed on his back several times a day hastened Longarm's healing. By the afternoon of the third day, he felt restless, ready to be up and around and doing his job again.

The truce between the cowboys and the timber men was holding, at least according to Matt Kinsman, who had come into Longarm's room at midday to see how he was doing. The rancher still didn't have a good word to say about Aurora, but he grudgingly admitted that the loggers had been keeping to themselves.

"They're stayin' on their lease, and my boys are stayin' on Diamond K range," Kinsman had said. "I got Joe ridin' close herd on all of 'em, just to make sure none of the young hellions get any foolish ideas in their heads."

That was a good idea, thought Longarm, and he told Kinsman as much. The cattleman just grunted, his naturally combative nature chafing under this enforced peace even though he had agreed to it.

Longarm's warbag and other gear had been brought into the house from the bunkhouse, and when Molly came into the spare bedroom later that afternoon, she found him standing up and buttoning the hickory-colored shirt he had taken from his bag. He already had his pants and boots on.

"What do you think you're doing?" she demanded, putting her hands on her hips, which were encased in snug denim trousers again today.

"Getting dressed so I can move around a mite," Longarm told her. "Fella like me gets cabin fever when he's cooped up for too long."

"You're in no shape—"

"Wing says that crease on my back has just about healed up," Longarm broke in, forestalling Molly's protest. "The bone and the muscles aren't near as sore as they were. No reason I can't get back to what brought me here in the first place."

"Only that you're liable to tear that wound open and bleed to death," said Molly bitterly.

Longarm grinned. "It ain't like I'm about to go out and wrassle a grizzle or anything. I'll be careful, Molly. No reason for you to worry about me."

She stepped closer to him, so close that he could almost feel the warmth coming from her, and said, "I haven't even talked you into making love to me yet, Custis. I don't want you going and dying."

Longarm cupped her chin and lifted her face so that he could look down into her eyes. "I don't intend dying any time soon," he said quietly. He moved his head closer, intending to brush his lips lightly across hers.

Instead, she grabbed him, her arms going around his neck and holding him tightly as she mashed her lips against his. She opened her mouth and her tongue slid boldly against his, exploring, probing, tantalizing. Longarm put his arms around her and felt the softness of her belly prodding urgently against his groin. Despite everything he had been through in the past week, enough of his strength had returned to him for his manhood to begin stiffening. Molly dropped one hand to it and began caressing and kneading the heavy length of him.

Longarm took his lips away from hers and said, "This ain't the time nor the place, Molly, but sometime . . ."

"You promise? Swear you'll do it." At that moment, she sounded more like a pleading little girl than the full-grown woman she really was.

Longarm nodded. "I swear."

She took a deep breath and disengaged herself from him. "All right. But I'll hold you to it, Custis. It was hard enough knowing that McEntire woman had bedded you when I thought I might never get the chance."

"Wait just a minute," Longarm said with a frown. "I don't know what you're—"

"Don't bother trying to deny it," she said blithely. "A woman can always tell. The way she was panting over you and wanting to take you back to her place, it was obvious."

Once again, Longarm was a little sorry he hadn't been awake to see the confrontation between Molly and Aurora. On the other hand, maybe it was a good thing he hadn't. Billy Vail already accused him of having a swelled head; seeing two beautiful women squabbling over him would've likely just made it worse.

As he reached for his gunbelt, he said to Molly, "Your pa

tells me there hasn't been any trouble since the other day."

"That's right," said Molly. "But it's been like waiting for a storm to break. You can tell something's going to happen. You just don't know when or how bad it's going to be."

Longarm knew what she meant. That was one reason he wanted to resume his investigation. He had to find out what was really going on around here before that storm broke.

Molly insisted on saddling the roan for him herself. Longarm halfway expected her to suggest that she go along with him, but she didn't, and he was thankful for that. Arguing with Molly could be downright tiring, and he needed all his strength right now.

Like Longarm, the roan was well rested and anxious to be doing something again. He had to hold the horse back a little as it pranced along the trail leading away from the Diamond K. Longarm knew what the situation was on the ranch; now he wanted to pay a visit to the logging camp and find out how things were going there.

He reached the main trail and swung south. The day was overcast but mild, with gray clouds that promised rain later on scudding through the sky. As Longarm neared the cutoff to the McEntire camp, he paused and listened for the sound of axes coming from higher on the mountain. The ringing of metal against wood came faintly to his ear, telling him that Aurora's men were hard at work.

He heard something else too—the squeaking of wagon wheels. A team of horses appeared at a bend in the trail ahead of him, and behind them came the wagon they were pulling. A lone man was seated on the wagon, handling the reins of the team. Longarm recognized him as the cook from Aurora's camp. That bald head was unmistakable.

Some instinct made Longarm rein his horse off the trail and into the trees. He didn't know if the cook had seen him or not, but if not, Longarm wanted to keep it that way. The wheels of his brain were clicking over a lot more quickly than those of the slow-moving camp wagon.

If the cook had been to town for supplies, which was the logical explanation for him being out in the wagon, where was he going now? He had already passed the turnoff that led to the logging camp.

Longarm swung down from the saddle and led the roan even deeper into the trees and brush. Suddenly it seemed very important that the cook not spot him when the wagon passed by on the trail.

Standing very still, Longarm watched through the screening brush as the wagon rolled past. He could keep track of its progress by the sound of its wheels and the clopping of its mule team's hooves. Once it had gone by him, Longarm turned and started making his way through the thick woods, still leading the roan. He was moving almost as fast on foot as the wagon.

Several minutes later, Longarm heard a different sound. Hoofbeats, but moving at a lighter, faster gait than the plodding of the mules. Someone else was riding along the trail. The squeaking of the wagon wheels stopped, and Longarm knew the cook must have halted the vehicle to let the rider come to him. Longarm angled toward the trail again, anxious to see just who Aurora's cook was rendezvousing with.

He didn't want the roan letting out a whinny at the wrong time, so he tied the horse's reins to a young pine and left it there, slipping closer to the trail on foot. He heard the hoofbeats of the rider's mount come to a halt. In a careful crouch, Longarm moved closer. He lifted a hand to ease aside some brush that blocked his view of the trail.

What he saw didn't really surprise him.

Ben Callahan, astride a big black horse, sat there talking to the cook from the McEntire logging camp.

Longarm felt his muscles tense. He had suspected almost from the first that whoever was behind Aurora's troubles had a man working for him in her camp. Now he had confirmation of that. There was no reason for this clandestine meeting unless the cook was passing on vital information to his real employer.

"What have you found out, Eli?" Callahan was saying.

The cook shook his bald head. "Not much, Boss. Miz McEntire's still all het up about something. Maybe because

116

that marshal fella is still over at the Diamond K, 'stead of with her.''

Longarm saw Callahan's face harden at the mention of him. ''That lawman's caused nothing but trouble,'' growled Callahan. ''It would've been all right with me if that ambush had killed him. I don't need him distracting Aurora right now.''

''You plan on makin' a move soon?''

''It looks like I'll have to,'' said Callahan grimly. ''Nothing else I've tried has worked. All I can do now is come after her with what she least expects.''

The cook chuckled. ''I reckon Miz McEntire'll be thrown for a loop, that's for sure. She won't know what hit her, Boss.''

Longarm felt rage building up inside him as he listened to the conversation. Callahan was behind all the mayhem that had infected this part of the woods, and now he was plotting his worst strike yet against Aurora. It was all Longarm could do not to pull his gun from its holster and burst out of the trees to arrest the bastard right here and now. He forced himself to keep listening, though, in hopes that Callahan would reveal something else important.

That wasn't meant to be. The sound of more riders came to Longarm's ears, and Callahan and the cook heard them too. Callahan's head lifted, and he said, ''Someone's coming. You get on back to camp, Eli. I'll talk to you again another time.''

''Sure thing, Boss.'' The cook began working to turn the wagon and the team around. Callahan wheeled his horse and rode back the way he had come, veering off the trail and into the woods before the approaching riders could sweep around a bend in the trail and spot him.

Not knowing who the riders were, Longarm had no choice but to stay where he was too. A couple of minutes later, they trotted past, about half a dozen of them, and Longarm recognized them as cowboys from the Diamond K. Seth Thomas was among them. Aurora's cook was still struggling with the wagon and the mules, and as the cowboys moved over to ride past him, they called out jeering comments. Even if they recognized the cook, thought Longarm, likely none of them would think anything about him being on a section of trail

117

where he had no real business being. The cowhands rode on out of sight, obviously bound for Timber City. A few moments later, the cook finally got the wagon turned around and whipped the mules into motion. The wagon rolled away toward the cutoff which would take it back to the McEntire camp.

Longarm straightened, wincing a little as muscles stiff from long minutes of crouching twinged in his legs and back. Anger still smoldered inside him. All that was left to do now was arrest Callahan, then gather up the cook too, because old Eli would probably be glad to testify against Callahan when he realized how much trouble he was in. With any luck, Longarm could wrap up this case today.

He went back to the roan, jerked the reins loose, and swung up into the saddle. He didn't know exactly where Ben Callahan's logging camp was, only that it was north of Aurora's operation and the Diamond K. Longarm thought he could find it fairly easily. All he had to do was follow the sound of axes.

About an hour later, after checking a couple of smaller trails that branched off the main one, Longarm found the path that led to Callahan's camp. Not only the ringing of axes but also the growl of a steam engine inside a small sawmill led him to his destination. Callahan's operation was smaller and less impressive than Aurora's, but as Longarm rode up to the camp, he noticed that the buildings and the equipment were well cared for, and there was an air of brisk efficiency about the place. Callahan had nothing to be ashamed of here.

Longarm noted another difference between Callahan's camp and Aurora's. There were no guards here—or if there were, they were so well hidden that Longarm couldn't spot them. But then, he reflected, Callahan didn't really need any guards. He hadn't encountered any of the problems that had been plaguing Aurora—because he was behind them.

That didn't stop a couple of the men who were working around the sawmill from picking up axes and strolling over to meet Longarm as he reined in. One of them, a burly fellow with a red beard, looked up at Longarm and asked, "What would ye be wantin' here, boyo?"

"I'm looking for Ben Callahan," Longarm answered bluntly. "Is he here?"

"Have business wi' him, do ye?"

"You could say that. I'm a U.S. deputy marshal, and I need to talk to Callahan."

The two loggers exchanged a glance, then Redbeard said, "So ye're the famous lawman we been hearin' so much about. Ye've come here t' put a stop t' all th' troubles."

"That's the general idea," said Longarm, growing impatient.

"And ye think Mr. Callahan can help ye?"

Longarm fixed the man with a cold stare. "I'm sure of it."

Before the loggers could say anything else, Callahan himself emerged from the sawmill. Longarm had expected Callahan to beat him back to the camp, since Longarm hadn't really known where he was going. Callahan glanced at Longarm in surprise, then said to the redbearded man, "What's going on here, Rory? Who is this man?"

"He's a badge-toter, he is, Mr. Callahan, an' he wants t' see you."

Callahan looked up at Longarm again. "You're that marshal I've heard about, the one who's working for Aurora McEntire."

Longarm suppressed a sigh of frustration. He wasn't surprised that news of his presence had spread through the mountains. After his part in stopping the battle between the Diamond K and the McEntire loggers, that was only to be expected. But it seemed like everybody around here was determined to jump to the wrong conclusions about him.

"I'm not working for Mrs. McEntire. I'm just trying to find out who's been causing trouble for her and Matt Kinsman," said Longarm. "I've got a few questions I want to ask you, Callahan."

The man shrugged his broad shoulders. "Sure. I don't know why you think I can help you, but if I can, I'd be glad to."

Callahan was a cool-headed son of a bitch, Longarm had to give him that. He had halfway expected Callahan to pull a gun upon being confronted like this. He had to suspect that Longarm was on to him.

119

Instead, Callahan turned away and said over his shoulder, "Come on in my shack, Marshal. We can talk there."

Frowning in puzzlement, Longarm swung down from the roan and handed the reins to Rory, who reached out for them. "I'll take care o' yer horse, Marshal," said the redbearded logger.

Longarm wasn't sure what was going on here, but he remained confident in his ability to handle whatever tricks Callahan had up his sleeve. He followed the boss logger into a small cabin that evidently served as Callahan's quarters.

The cabin was furnished with a table and a couple of chairs, a bunk, and a sturdy trunk that sat at the foot of the bed. Callahan opened the trunk and took out a bottle. "Care for a drink, Marshal?" he asked.

Longarm saw to his surprise that the label on the bottle proclaimed it to be Maryland rye, Tom Moore to be precise. What were the odds that Callahan would have a bottle of Longarm's favorite here in the middle of the Cascades?

It had been a long time since he had asked too many questions of such good fortune, however. He could arrest Callahan *after* they'd had a drink just as well as before. With a nod, he said, "Much obliged."

Callahan dug a couple of glasses out of the trunk, blew dust from them, and pulled the cork from the bottle of rye with his teeth. He splashed liquor into each glass, then replaced the bottle in the trunk and held out one of the glasses to Longarm. Longarm was about to toss off the drink when Callahan lifted his own glass and said, "Here's to Aurora McEntire."

Longarm nodded curtly and said, "To Aurora." Then he downed the rye, licked his lips appreciatively, and went on. "You always drink to somebody you're trying to run out of business, Callahan?"

Callahan frowned, taken aback by the blunt question. "What are you talking about, Marshal? I wouldn't want to hurt Aurora's business."

"No, you just want to make things so bad for her that she'll sell out to you on the cheap, government contract and all."

Callahan's blunt fingers tightened on the empty glass he held. "You're insane," he said. "I'd never hurt Aurora."

Longarm's right hand was close to the butt of his Colt, just in case Callahan decided to try something funny. "That ain't the way I figure it," he said coldly. "You see, I was there a few days ago when you offered to buy her out. You practically admitted you were behind all her troubles. And I saw you meeting on the sly today with her cook, who's been helping you with your scheme."

For a long moment, Callahan stared hard at Longarm. Then he shook his head sadly. "You don't understand, Marshal," he said. "You just don't understand."

"Then why don't you explain it to me?" Longarm snapped.

Callahan looked down at the cabin's puncheon floor and heaved a sigh, then said, "All right. If I have to." His gaze lifted, and his eyes met Longarm's. "I don't really want to buy Aurora out. I'm in love with her, and I want to marry her."

Chapter 11

This time it was Longarm's turn to stare in amazement. Of all the things Callahan might have said, that was one of the last ones Longarm would have expected.

"Marry her?" he repeated. "You don't even like her. Aurora told me how you broke up your partnership with Angus McEntire because he decided to marry her and you couldn't stand her."

A look of pure misery appeared on Callahan's face. "That's what she thinks? I ended my partnership with Angus because I couldn't stand knowing that Aurora was marrying him instead of me. I knew if Angus and I stayed partners, I'd have to see her sometimes, and that was more than I could take."

Longarm was flabbergasted by this agonized confession on Callahan's part and not sure whether to believe the man or not. He said, "Didn't you ever tell Aurora how you really felt about her?"

Callahan shook his head. "She was happy with Angus. I couldn't bring myself to cause trouble for her. I suppose you could say I just . . . loved her from afar."

122

"Maybe *you* could say something like that," muttered Longarm. "I couldn't." He glared at Callahan and went on. "What about that fella Eli, that bald-headed cook? Like I told you, I saw the two of you—"

Callahan held up both hands, palms out. "I know, I know. And I admit that Eli has been working for me. But not because I want to cause trouble for Aurora. I just had Eli there to keep an eye on her, so that I would know what was going on. When I first heard about the problems she was having, I figured it was time to make my move. I offered to buy her company from her."

"So, you don't want to cause trouble for her, but you don't mind taking advantage of trouble she's already got, is that it?" asked Longarm skeptically.

Callahan grimaced. "You make it sound pretty bad, Marshal, but you don't know everything I had in mind. I thought it would be better for Aurora if she didn't have to worry about the company anymore. I thought too that if maybe whoever was behind the problems had a grudge against her, he would stop if the company changed hands. Then I was going to . . . to ask Aurora to marry me, so that I could give the company back to her as a wedding present."

That was one of the craziest things Longarm had ever heard, but he had to admit that it was just the sort of thing a lovesick fool such as Callahan professed to be might come up with. Still, he wasn't ready to write off his suspicions just yet.

"I heard you tell Eli that you were going to try something new with Aurora, since nothing else had worked, and that old cook said she wouldn't know what hit her. What was *that* about?"

"I was talking about the way I've been trying to buy her out," said Callahan. "If you were eavesdropping outside the cabin the other day, you know I made my final offer to Aurora, and she turned me down flat."

Longarm nodded.

"So there's nothing else left to do," said Callahan with another shrug. "If I can't buy her out before I propose, I guess I'll just have to go ahead and ask her to marry me anyway.

That was what Eli and I were talking about, Marshal. You can ask him if you don't believe me.''

Longarm wasn't sure why Callahan thought he was more likely to believe the old cook. Callahan was either one hell of an actor, or he was really telling the truth about his involvement with the situation. Longarm had been counting on the man panicking when confronted with the knowledge of his guilt. That hadn't worked out at all.

And Longarm was once again left with no solid proof of anything.

"All right, Callahan," he said abruptly. "I ain't saying I believe this yarn you've spun for me, but I reckon you know I've got my eye on you now. We'll just see what happens."

"I've told you the truth, Marshal." A trace of fire appeared in Callahan's gaze. Now that he had gotten over the awkwardness of being forced to confess his love for Aurora, his normal spirit was coming back to him. "If you don't want to believe me, that's *your* problem."

"We'll see," said Longarm. "Thanks for the drink." He turned toward the door of the cabin.

"That's it?" asked Callahan in surprise. "You're leaving?"

"Not much else I can do, is there? Not unless you want to confess that you tried to have me killed and caused all that trouble around the McEntire camp."

Callahan shook his head vehemently. "I didn't have anything to do with any of that."

Longarm just raised one eyebrow skeptically and stepped out of the cabin.

The roan was tied to a hitching post nearby. Longarm untied the reins and stepped up into the saddle. Callahan came out of the cabin behind him, and although Longarm didn't look back as he rode away from the camp, he could feel the boss logger watching him. Callahan's eyes seemed to bore into his back.

He had put Callahan on notice, and if the man was indeed guilty, it was now just a matter of giving the man enough rope to hang himself.

And of staying alive in the meantime, Longarm added grimly to himself.

• • •

He had been heading for the McEntire camp when he had gotten sidetracked on this Callahan business, so that was where he pointed the roan when he reached the main trail once more. The skin on the back of his neck crawled a little as he rode. Callahan might move fast to eliminate him as a threat. Even now, some of those hired gunmen might be riding through the forest to get in front of him and set up an ambush. Or they might just come straight after him and try to ride him down. Either way, Longarm knew he had to be alert for any sign of trouble.

Nothing happened on the way to Aurora's headquarters, however. When Longarm rode up there, everything was evidently business as usual. The sawmill was operating, and Longarm saw a boom of logs floating down the creek. Some of the timbermen known as river pigs were controlling it with long poles and ropes that had been attached to the iron spikes called dogs that had been driven into the outer logs of the boom. Those outer logs were strung end to end and attached to each other to form a ring that contained the rest of the logs. The river pigs were good at their job and floated the boom gently up to the big open end of the sawmill building that extended out over the water. This boom was not going to get away and cause trouble.

The only thing Longarm noticed that was unusual was the level of the creek. It seemed to have dropped, though there was still enough water in the stream to float the boom with no trouble. There wouldn't be if the creek went down much more.

Longarm resolved to satisfy his curiosity and ask Aurora about that, but first he wanted to make certain she was all right and that there had been no trouble here in his absence. He brought the roan to a stop and dismounted, looping the reins around the hitching post in front of Aurora's cabin.

Jared Flint answered his knock on the door instead of Aurora. The foreman said, "Hello, Marshal. Finally get enough of Kinsman's hospitality?"

Longarm had sensed all along that Flint didn't particularly like him, so the man's attitude came as no surprise. Also, the

125

hatred between the loggers and the cattlemen ran so deep and strong that the slightest appearance of favoring one side over the other was enough to make enemies. Longarm didn't let it worry him. He just asked, "Is Mrs. McEntire here?"

Aurora must have already heard Flint's greeting to him, because she appeared at the foreman's shoulder and said, "Custis! Are you all right? Have you recovered from that wound?"

"Pretty much," Longarm said. He stepped forward, and Flint had no choice but to move aside and let him into the cabin. He ignored the bushy-browed glower Flint gave him and went on to Aurora. "I figured I'd better see how things were going here."

"It's been quiet," she told him. "If it stayed this peaceful all the time, we wouldn't have any trouble meeting the terms of that contract. We've already made up some of the time and timber we lost. And thanks to some of Mr. Flint's ideas, we're going to make up the rest of it."

Longarm looked at Flint quizzically, and the man said, "You might not understand, Marshal."

"I've been around a few logging operations before," Longarm said mildly. "This wouldn't have anything to do with the way the creek's gone down some, would it?"

"As a matter of fact, it does," said Aurora. "We've dammed off one of the tributaries that feeds into the creek higher up the mountain. When it forms a big enough pond, we're going to build a log flume from it down here to the mill. We can still float booms down the creek from the lower slopes the way we've been doing, but when we're finished with the flume we can go ahead and start cutting on the higher slopes too, and shoot the logs down that way. We'll be working on two sections of the mountain at once, instead of just one."

"That'll take more men," Longarm pointed out.

"Already hired 'em," said Flint. "They built that dam, and they've started the upper end of the flume."

Longarm nodded. If everything went as Aurora and Flint planned, the camp's production would indeed increase. Pretty soon, the sawmill might be running twenty-four hours a day.

That would make the McEntire timber operation a mighty

tempting target for somebody who wanted to take it over. Somebody like Ben Callahan, say . . .

Longarm kept those thoughts to himself. He knew from experience that Aurora didn't want to believe the worst of Callahan. Nor did he say anything about old Eli, the cook, being on Callahan's payroll. He preferred that Callahan's spy stay in place here in Aurora's camp—although now that Callahan knew Longarm suspected him, he might order Eli to hightail it out of there. Either way, Longarm was going to wait and see what happened. He believed that Aurora and her people were relatively safe for the moment. *He* himself represented the biggest threat to the mastermind, be it Callahan or somebody else. He was more likely to be the target of whatever happened next.

"And speakin' of that flume, I'd better go see how the boys are doing," Flint went on. "I'll let you know later, Miz McEntire."

"All right, Mr. Flint," said Aurora. She waited until the foreman was gone, then turned to Longarm and said eagerly, "You're spending the night here, aren't you?"

Longarm hesitated before saying, "All my gear's at the Diamond K, and they're expecting me back. Under the circumstances, as long as you folks are getting along, I don't want to give anybody any excuses for starting a ruckus."

Aurora's lips thinned. "You think that if you don't go back to the little redhead hellcat she's liable to bring some of those cowboys up here looking for you?"

"I reckon it might sound a little immodest," said Longarm with a grin, "but that could happen, all right."

"Very well," Aurora said coolly. "Go on back to the Diamond K. But I want you to know what you're going to be missing."

She stepped closer to him, and her hand went to his groin, cupping and caressing. Startled, Longarm said, "Hold on a minute."

Her fingers tightened on him through the fabric of his trousers. "That's just what I intend to do," she said with a smile that was half-angel, half-devil. She stroked his stiffening man-

127

hood for a moment, until it bulged out against the front of his denims.

Longarm expected her to just tease him a mite to let him know how put out she was with him for not staying at the lumber camp, but instead she began unfastening the buttons of his trousers. Her hand delved inside, and her smooth, cool fingers found the fevered length of him. Deftly, she extricated his shaft, and Longarm growled deep in his throat as the pole of flesh sprang free.

Aurora used both hands to stroke him now. She looked down and licked her lips. "There's something I've always wanted to do," she said quietly. "Angus was too stiff-necked for it, bless his heart. He was a good man, but not the most adventurous lover."

At the moment, Longarm didn't particularly want to hear about Aurora's late husband. Not with the swelling length of his manhood filling both her hands. "You just go ahead and do whatever it is you want to do," he told her hoarsely. "I was raised to be a gentleman, and a gentleman always accommodates a lady."

Again she licked her lips. "You may not think I'm a lady when I get through with you," she said.

Then she dropped to her knees in front of him, opened her mouth wide, and closed her lips around the head of his shaft.

Longarm tried not to groan too loud as she started sucking. He could believe that she had never given any French lessons, because she went right for the final stretch instead of pacing herself. "No offense," he said in a husky voice, "but I reckon it'd be more fun for both of us if you'd slow down a mite."

She took her lips away, and his shaft throbbed with the loss of the wet heat that had been enfolding it. Aurora whispered, "You mean . . . like this?"

Her tongue darted out of her mouth, flicking tiny, butterfly-like blows against his burning flesh. She moved all around the head, maddeningly slowly, then used the tip of her tongue to toy with the slit at the end of his pole. Eagerly, she lapped up the clear juices that were seeping from the opening. When Longarm thought he couldn't stand any more of that without going completely insane, she stopped and began raining kisses on him, trailing them down the veined underside of his shaft and then back along the side. Her tongue came out again and licked him in long, slathering swipes.

Longarm wouldn't call any woman a liar unless she proved it to him. So he was willing to give Aurora the benefit of the doubt and believe that right now was the first time in her life she had ever done this.

But if that was the case, she sure as hell had a natural-born talent for it.

Once again she took him into her mouth, and as she did so, he began stroking her dark hair. Her head bobbed up and down over his groin. His legs, spread wide on the floor for balance, shook as tremors of passionate sensation ran through them. He felt as if his strength might desert him at any moment, leaving him helpless to keep from falling flat on his face, but somehow it didn't happen. The insistent embrace of Aurora's lips strengthened him. As he felt his climax boiling up from deep within him, he put one hand on her shoulder and the other on the back of her head. To steady herself, she reached around behind him and clutched his backside, digging her fingers into it.

It was as if both of them were aware of the explosion coming and knew they had better hold on for dear life.

Involuntarily, Longarm's hips twitched as culmination shook him. Aurora moaned and swallowed eagerly as Longarm's pearlescent seed raced along the length of his shaft and burst out into her mouth. Spasm after spasm rocked him as he spurted. The moment seemed to stretch out endlessly. He wouldn't have suspected that he had that much to give her.

And she took it avidly, every drop, squeezing the last bit from him and swirling her tongue around his softening shaft to make sure none had escaped her.

Longarm closed his eyes and dropped his head forward. Blood thundered inside his head from his racing pulse. In his life, many women had done for him what Aurora had just done.

But few if any had ever done it any better.

"That was . . . mighty fine," he said when he had recovered a little of his breath.

Aurora looked up at him and licked her lips one last time. "I did it all right?" she asked.

Longarm took hold of her shoulders and lifted her to her feet. "More than all right," he told her. "If you were any better at it, you'd have likely killed me."

Aurora gave a little laugh and hugged him. "I wouldn't want that." She reached down, tucked him away, and buttoned his trousers again. "I suppose if you really have to go back to the Diamond K now, at least you'll remember me."

"I'm not likely to ever forget," Longarm said sincerely.

"But next time—and there *will* be a next time—it's going to be *my* turn. Dear Angus was a bit squeamish about other things too."

Longarm could just imagine—and that was his problem. In his mind's eye, he saw Aurora spread out there on that bed, splendidly nude, creamy thighs flung wide open, the patch of dark hair and the inviting folds of pink flesh that it framed calling out to him with an urgency that would not be denied. That vision was probably exactly what she had meant for him to see, he thought.

"Next time," agreed Longarm. "You've got my word on that."

"And I'll hold you to it," said Aurora. She kissed him, then said, "All right. Go."

It was only as Longarm was riding away from the camp that he recalled the conversation he'd had with Molly Kinsman earlier in the day, before leaving the Diamond K. He had made a promise to her too, and she had responded in exactly the same words as Aurora.

I'll hold you to it.

Longarm shook his head in chagrin.

There were times when being a man of his word could be downright tiring—and he suspected that where Aurora and Molly were concerned, this was going to be one of those times.

Chapter 12

As Longarm more than halfway expected, Molly Kinsman was waiting for him when he got back to the Diamond K. She came down rapidly from the porch, where she had been standing with her hands on the railing, and hurried out to meet him as he rode up.

"Did you have any trouble?" she asked anxiously.

Longarm shook his head. "Nary a bit." For the time being, he wasn't going to mention his suspicions of Ben Callahan, or the confrontation he'd had today with the man, to anyone on the Diamond K. There would be time enough for that when he had proof one way or the other.

"Did you see *her*?"

Wisely, Longarm refrained from grinning. But it was difficult, because the memory of what Aurora had done to him was still incredibly vivid in his mind. Instead, as he dismounted he said noncommittally, "As a matter of fact, I did. I talked to Mrs. McEntire and her foreman and found out they haven't had any trouble since the truce they called with your father. Heard about their plans for expanding their operation too.''

Molly rolled her eyes in disgust. ''That's all we need, more trees cut down on the mountains. Do you know what that will do to the runoff and the soil erosion around here?''

''Well, from what I've seen so far, Mrs. McEntire and her men are being careful not to clear-cut too much land,'' said Longarm as he led the roan into the barn. ''A lot of those logging companies don't give a damn what kind of shape they leave the country in behind them, but that ain't true of Mrs. McEntire and her men. I don't think you have to worry over-much about what they're doing ruining your range.''

''I hope you're right,'' said Molly, ''but I'll believe it when I see it.''

Longarm unsaddled the roan, rubbed it down, and turned it into its usual stall. Molly pitched in to help him, forking up some hay and carrying it over to the stall. They were alone in the barn at the moment, but it was late afternoon and Longarm knew that wouldn't last. Soon, the hands would be drifting in from their day's work, and they would want to put their horses up. Longarm hoped Molly realized that.

If she did, she didn't care. She stepped up to him and put her hands on his arms. ''Custis,'' she said softly, ''you made a promise to me.''

''I know I did, Molly,'' said Longarm, his voice solemn, ''but surely you don't expect me to honor it right here and now! Hell, girl, anybody could walk in on us—that young firebrand Seth, or Joe Traywick, or your daddy. Any one of 'em would be liable to up and shoot me if they caught us.''

Molly turned away, pouting. ''You just don't want me because you probably spent the afternoon romping with *her*.''

She could pack an awful lot of scorn into one little word, thought Longarm. But he wasn't just about to tell her how close to the truth she was.

Besides, it hadn't been *all* afternoon. . . .

He put a hand on Molly's shoulder. ''I'm not trying to put you off,'' he said gently. ''It's like I told you—''

''I know, the right time and place.'' Her voice was dull now. It became a little more spirited as she went on. ''If you're

132

not careful, Custis, I might just decide that making love with you isn't such a good idea after all.''

''That'd be up to you,'' he said honestly.

Molly gave him a long, searching look, then turned and walked out of the barn. Longarm waited a minute or two, giving her time to get back into the house, then followed. He turned toward the bunkhouse rather than the main house, though. He wanted to talk to Joe Traywick.

Traywick was out on the range somewhere, which came as no surprise to Longarm. He sat down on a stool in front of the bunkhouse and picked up a piece of branch from the ground. Drawing his clasp knife, he opened the blade and began shaving thin curls of wood off the broken branch. To the casual observer, it would look like he was simply whittling to pass the time. In reality, though, Longarm was thinking, replaying and turning over in his mind everything that had happened since his arrival in the Cascades a week or so earlier.

Those rustled steers still bothered him. It had taken a cowboy to pull that off. But the accidents that had struck Aurora's logging operation had to have been carried out by a timber man. It was unlikely any of the Diamond K hands would have known how to rig a high topper's pulley so that it would plunge the timber cutter to his death. Nor would they be overly familiar with the booms of logs floating down the creek and know how to send one of them careening out of control.

Could there be *two* bunches of badmen causing trouble around here?

Longarm considered that possibility for several moments, then tentatively discarded it. Everything pointed to the fact that someone was trying to play the McEntire Timber Company and the Diamond K against each other. Longarm's instincts told him that one person was behind the trouble, one schemer who was perfectly capable of hiring both renegade loggers and drifting hardcases with cowboy skills to carry out his plans.

The knife blade practically flew over the wood as Longarm whittled and thought, thought and whittled.

He was on to something, he sensed. If Callahan was the culprit, he could recruit some of his own men to attack the McEntire operation, but he would still need some place for

133

the owlhoots he had hired to hole up whenever they weren't creating more deadly mischief on the Diamond K. And even if Callahan wasn't involved, whoever the boss was would still have to have a hiding place for his men. Some place handy, where he could get word to them fairly quickly.

Longarm turned his head, looking up at the peaks of the Cascades rising above this lower valley. Somewhere up there was the place where the troublemakers lurked, awaiting the word from their mysterious boss so that they could ride out and bring death and destruction once more to those in their path. Longarm's fingers clenched tightly on the clasp knife.

There was a little matter of a couple of bushwhackings too. The attempts on his life had come before anyone on the Diamond K knew who he really was. That was important, and he realized now that he had tried to grasp that fact several days earlier, as he was going to sleep in the spare bedroom of the ranch house following the meal Wing had brought to him. No one on the ranch—not Kinsman or Traywick, or Seth Thomas, or any of the other hands, no matter how young and hot-headed—had had any reason to try to have him killed so early on in the game. Seth held a grudge against him, sure ... but the young cowboy would have tried to settle it himself, not hired a backshooter. Longarm was sure of that.

Which left Callahan as the only logical suspect. Callahan had a spy in the McEntire camp; that was beyond dispute. Eli could have told Callahan that a federal lawman was poking around, and Callahan could have issued orders to have that potentially thorny problem nipped in the bud—with a bullet.

But despite everything that pointed to Callahan, there was still one problem: The man had an explanation for his actions, and one that could even be considered halfway logical if you made allowances for how love could addle a man's mind.

Longarm kept coming back to the fact that the gang, no matter who their boss was, had to have a place to hide out. Those stolen cows had gone *somewhere*. Why not up into the mountains, to some isolated high valley? Some place above the Diamond K range, maybe along the border between the timber leases of Aurora McEntire and Ben Callahan. It was possible.

Longarm knew he was going to have to find out for sure.

He was deep in those thoughts when a familiar voice asked, "What you carvin' there, Custis?"

Longarm looked up and saw Traywick standing there in front of him. Then he glanced at the branch in his hand, which he had whittled down to practically nothing while he was thinking. There was only a thin length of pale white pine left. Longarm grinned and said, "Reckon it's an albino snake."

Traywick hooked another stool with his foot, drew it over, and sat down wearily. "You ought to see the things one of our hands named Hank can whittle. Boy carved out a little bitty Studebaker wagon once. Wheels turned and the wagon tongue went up and down, just like a real one." The ranch foreman shook his head. "Boy's got a gift."

"I've been thinking, Joe," said Longarm, changing the subject. "You've been in this part of the country for a long time, haven't you?"

Traywick nodded. "Man and boy, nigh onto thirty years. I've ridden over most of it."

"Are there any places high up in the mountains, maybe just under the timberline, where a group of men could hole up, maybe even keep a small herd of cattle?"

"You're thinkin' of that stock we had rustled back when this whole mess started, ain't you?"

"Those cows had to go somewhere," Longarm pointed out. "And those cowboys who raided the lumber camp have to have some place to hide too."

Slowly, Traywick nodded. "I suppose there are some places that fit the bill. We never really went lookin' because—" He abruptly fell silent.

"Because you just figured that Aurora McEntire and her men were to blame," Longarm finished.

"Made sense at the time," Traywick muttered with a shrug.

"Think I'll take a ride up into the mountains tomorrow," Longarm said. "See what I can find if I look around a mite."

Traywick glanced over at him. "Want some company?"

"I'd like that, Joe," said Longarm. "Reckon I'd like that just fine."

• • •

As it turned out, though, Joe Traywick didn't ride with him. Longarm planned to start early, before dawn, and as he walked toward the barn in the grayness of approaching day, he heard yelling from inside the big building. A moment later, Traywick came hopping through the open double doors. Longarm hurried over to him to steady him.

"What happened?"

"Son-of-a-bitchin' horse stomped the hell out of my foot," Traywick groaned. "My boot's full of blood, Custis."

"Come on, let's get you in the house."

Longarm helped Traywick to the back door of the ranch house, knowing that Wing was already up and about in the kitchen. Wing took one look at the foreman's gray, haggard face and exclaimed in Chinese. "Don't start talkin' that gibberish," said Traywick as Longarm helped him sit down at the table, "nor that pidgin English neither. I know you can talk as good as anybody on the ranch, Wing, maybe better."

Wing gave a mock sigh. "Can a man have no secrets around here?" he asked rhetorically. "What in Tophet happened to you, Joe?"

"Horse stomped my foot."

"Let's get that boot off and take a look at it."

As Traywick had said, his boot was full of blood from the ugly gash that had been opened across the top of his foot. Wing examined the wound after carefully working the boot off and cutting away Traywick's blood-soaked sock. "You're going to be laid up for a good spell, Joe," said the cook solemnly. "I can sew up that cut, or we can take you to the doc in Timber City if you want. You've likely got some broken bones in there too."

Traywick shook his head. "You take care of it, Wing," he said. "I trust you more'n I do any sawbones from town. You've been patchin' us up for a long time around here."

"All too true," agreed Wing. "I'll need some whiskey."

"You and me both," grunted Traywick.

A new voice came from the doorway of the kitchen. "My God, Joe, what happened?" Molly Kinsman rushed into the room, wrapped in a long blue robe. Her hair hung loose around

136

her shoulders, not yet brushed after her night's sleep, and Longarm thought she looked mighty pretty.

He had other things on his mind besides appreciating how lovely Molly was, however. As Traywick launched into yet another explanation of what had happened to him, and Wing and Molly fussed over him, Longarm eased out the back door of the house. He still had work to do.

During their conversation of the day before, Traywick had told him quite a bit about the lay of the land higher up in the mountains. Though he would have felt better about things with Traywick guiding him—and backing him up in case of trouble—Longarm felt confident he could find the places Traywick had told him about. He was sure he could get one of the other hands to ride with him, but there were none of them he trusted as much as he did Traywick. Besides, it was his job to run those badmen to ground, and he didn't really have the right to expose anyone else to the danger that might be awaiting him.

No, he would go it alone, he decided. Wouldn't be the first time he had played a lone hand, and it probably wouldn't be the last.

In the dim light of the lantern he lit in the barn, he saddled the roan and then led the horse outside. The sky was still just turning gray to the east. The rest of the hands would be rising soon, and Longarm wanted to be gone before then. He had plenty of riding to do today. He swung up into the saddle and heeled the roan into a trot.

The rising sun found Longarm high on the mountain that loomed directly above the Diamond K. He was cutting through part of the McEntire timber lease, but it was a section the loggers had not yet reached. He was far enough away from Aurora's current operation that he couldn't even hear the axes of the men as they began their day's work. In fact, he might as well have been alone on the mountain, save for the birds that flitted from pine to pine and the small animals that rustled away through the underbrush at his approach. A chattering noise made him look up, and he grinned at a squirrel that sat perched on a branch about twenty feet over his head, scolding him. Suddenly, something bounced off Longarm's hat and rolled to a stop on the forest floor.

"Better watch it, old son," he told the squirrel. "You keep throwing pine cones at me, we're liable to have us some squirrel stew for supper tonight."

With a defiant flip of its bushy red tail, the squirrel bounded off the branch, leaping easily to another one and then vanishing among the pine boughs.

Longarm chuckled and rode on. All of his problems should be so easily solved, he thought.

As the sun rose higher, the vegetation began to thin somewhat. In places, Longarm could look up and see the bare rock of the mountain peaks. Nothing grew up there except some lichen and moss. It was always cold at those elevations too, no matter what the weather was down below. In fact, there was already a chilly breeze playing around him, but Longarm wasn't bothered enough by it to reach into his saddlebags and pull out the jacket he had rolled up and put there. He just tugged his Stetson down a little tighter on his head and rode on.

Around mid-morning, he found himself at the lower end of a deep coulee that ran almost straight up the side of the mountain. The slope was fairly steep, but the roan was surefooted. Longarm felt confident that the horse could make it. The floor of the coulee was littered with small boulders and dead brush that had washed down during heavy rains. The sky was clear today, with only a few white puffballs of cloud floating here and there, and no threat of a storm. Still, Longarm felt a prickle of nervousness as he started up the coulee. He had seen more than one flash flood in his time, and he knew how quickly gullies like this could turn into raging torrents.

He recognized the coulee from his conversation with Joe Traywick the day before, though, and knew from what the ranch foreman had told him that this was the quickest and best way to the upper reaches of the mountain. Longarm kept the roan moving, letting the mount set its own pace and pick its own way.

As he rode, Longarm kept an eye on the rocky ground. After a few minutes, he reined the horse to a stop and swung down from the saddle to kneel beside a small, silvery mark on the stone floor of the coulee. Only a keen observer would have ever noticed it. Longarm touched the mark lightly with his finger.

A horseshoe had scraped the rock here, Longarm knew. He looked a little farther on, and saw a small stone that appeared to have been overturned recently. Riders moving through this coulee, especially if they were careful, would leave few if any tracks.

But even the most careful riders could overlook tiny signs of their presence like these. It would take a sharp-eyed tracker to spot them . . . but Longarm had been taught to read sign by some of the best in the world: Apaches, Arapahos, Crows. By the time he mounted again and rode another half mile or so, he was certain that a good-sized group of horsemen had ridden through this coulee several times recently.

His pulse quickened. He was on the trail of the hired killers who worked for the man behind all the trouble down below. He was sure of it.

As he neared the upper end of the coulee, it began to twist and turn. Longarm proceeded carefully around the bends in the natural passage. It was conceivable that the hired guns would have posted guards, though he figured they probably felt pretty safe way up here on the mountain like this. Still, he didn't want to ride into another ambush.

Suddenly, the small sound of metal clinking on stone made him rein in and stiffen in the saddle. The noise had come from *behind* him, rather than in front of him, as he might have expected. He listened intently, and heard a few more little sounds that told him he was definitely being followed.

Grim-faced, Longarm slid down from the roan's saddle and led the horse around another bend in the coulee. There was a good-sized boulder here that jutted out from the side of the gully. Longarm hid the roan behind it, then began climbing the rough, sloping face of the big rock. When he got to the top, he would be able to look down on the primitive trail and see whoever was following him.

The noises came closer, and he was able to identify them positively now as hoofbeats. The mysterious tracker seemed to be trying to be quiet, but he wasn't very good at it. Longarm waited patiently.

The rider came into view, wearing a sheepskin jacket and a flat-crowned hat. Longarm caught only a glimpse of him before he started around the big rock on which Longarm crouched. The lawman twisted around and drew his Colt. If the rider kept moving—and there was no reason to think that he wouldn't—in a moment or two he would emerge so that once more Longarm could cover him.

That was what happened. Longarm straightened as the rider rounded the upthrust rock. The sound of a shot would echo far up the mountain, so Longarm didn't want to use the Colt unless he had to. Instead, he slid down the rock face a short distance and used his momentum to launch himself into space.

His dive carried him across the open space between himself and his mysterious follower. Longarm crashed heavily into the man, knocking him out of the saddle. They both fell, and Longarm grunted in pain as the impact of landing on the hard, rocky ground sent flashes of pain through his injured back. He didn't feel any wetness against his skin, however, so he thought the gash across his back hadn't opened up and started bleeding again.

The fellow he had jumped seemed to be stunned. Longarm scrambled up, still holding the gun, and used his free hand to grab the man's shoulder. As he rolled the follower over, the man's hat came loose.

And long red spilled out from under it.

Longarm bit back a curse. He was looking down into the face of Molly Kinsman.

He should have expected that, Longarm told himself as he stood up. Molly moved her head back and forth a little and moaned. She was stunned, all right, but she was coming around. Her eyelids fluttered open, and she looked up at Longarm in confusion.

"What . . . what happened?"

He sighed and reached down to give her a hand as she struggled to sit up. "Reckon I could ask you the same thing," he said. "What are you doing here, Molly? How'd you come to be following me?"

Slowly, she got to her feet. "Joe told me what you were doing today," she said. "He even told me where I was likely to find you. I took a few shortcuts."

"Blast it! I told Traywick I didn't want him blabbing to anybody about what we had planned."

Molly smiled. "Oh. Well, that was a waste of time, Custis. Joe's never been able to keep a secret from me."

Longarm grunted. He could just imagine. Molly probably had Traywick wrapped completely around her little finger. Likely she hadn't even had to try very hard to worm Longarm's destination out of him.

"Joe said you shouldn't have started up here by yourself," Molly went on, "and since I've ridden over every foot of this mountain a dozen times since I was a little girl, I thought I'd come lend a hand." She gestured toward the upper end of the coulee. "There's a little valley up there, just like you asked Joe about. Men could stay there, and they could hide stolen cattle there too. And that's not the only place. I know several more spots that might make good hideouts for somebody."

Longarm shook his head. "I want you to get right back on that horse and head back down to the ranch," he told her sternly. "Hunting outlaws and hired guns is no place for you."

"That's not fair," she protested, once again sounding like a little kid. "I can help you, Custis."

"Don't want your help," he said flatly. He might have to offend her in order to get her to leave, but it would be worth it.

Molly's face hardened as she looked at him. "You don't seem to want any of the things I've offered you," she said slowly. "I practically throw myself at you over and over again, and you keep shooing me away like I'm nothing more than a bratty little pest!"

Longarm shrugged eloquently.

"Oh! So that is what you think of me! Well, I'll show you, Mr. High and Mighty U.S. Marshal!" Her hands went to the collar of her flannel shirt under the open sheepskin jacket, and a quick, hard tug popped several of the buttons as she ripped the shirt open. "There! Does that look like I'm a kid?"

She had bared her breasts, small, firm, pear-shaped cones

141

that were lightly dusted with freckles. They were tipped with pale brown nipples that puckered from the chilly air, or arousal, or both. Longarm had to admit that as breasts went, they were a mighty pert and appealing pair.

Still, he didn't think it would be wise—not to mention comfortable—to lay her down on the floor of this rocky coulee and take his pleasure with her. "Molly," he began, "I know I made you a promise—"

"Yes, you did," she broke in, "and it's time you kept it! You make love to me, here and now, and . . . and, well, I'll go back to the ranch like you want me to."

"And if I don't?" Longarm asked ominously.

Calmly, Molly replied, "Then I start screaming. And sound carries a long way up here, Custis. If the men you're looking for are really up there higher on the mountain, they're liable to hear me, and then you won't be able to sneak up on them."

Longarm stared at her for a long moment, his eyes narrowing in anger at being blackmailed like this. Then, abruptly, a chuckle came from him. He couldn't help but admire somebody with as much gall as Molly Kinsman seemed to possess.

As if sensing that he was weakening, she added quickly, "Anyway, up here you don't have to worry about anybody seeing us. No one will ever have to know."

"All right," said Longarm. "But not right here. Too damn many rocks. Is there any grass in that little valley you mentioned?"

Molly nodded eagerly. "Sure. Grass and trees. It's one of the nicest spots you'll ever see, Custis."

"Let's go take a look then. If there aren't any outlaws hiding there, I reckon we can see about getting what we both want. Just close up that shirt until then, all right?"

Grinning, Molly pulled the ripped shirt together over her breasts. As they mounted up, however, Longarm noticed that it didn't cover her very well anymore. One or both of those hard nipples kept peeking out impishly.

It took another ten minutes to reach the upper end of the coulee. Longarm made Molly stay back while he catfooted ahead to check it out, Winchester held ready in his hands. The little valley ran crossways at the top of the gully, like the bar of a letter T. It was perhaps a hundred yards long and fifty wide, and Longarm could see the whole place as he edged his head above the lip of the coulee. As Molly had said, there were several clumps of pines and a thin coating of grass on the ground. Longarm saw no signs of hired guns or stolen cattle or anybody else, for that matter. He and Molly had the place to themselves.

"Come on up," he told her as he turned and gestured for her to proceed. "If the hideout's up here, it must be in one of those other spots you mentioned."

"I'll show them to you," she offered as she came up even with him.

"You'll tell me how to find them," said Longarm, his tone brooking no argument. "You agreed to go back down the mountain, remember?"

"Only when we're through making love," she reminded him—as if he was likely to forget.

He let her pick the place. She chose a little hollow beneath the spreading branches of a cluster of pines. At this elevation, the trees were somewhat shorter and not as thick through their trunks. The true giants prized so highly by the loggers grew lower down on the slopes. But these were good-sized trees, and they made a shady bower around Longarm and Molly.

When they had tied their horses so that the mounts could graze on the thin grass, she stood before him and gave a toss of her head that made her long red hair swirl around her shoulders. "Undress me," she said.

"You're liable to get a mite cold," Longarm warned her.

Molly shook her head. "No. I'm already hot."

He knew what she meant. That torn shirt had spread open again, and his eyes were drawn back to her breasts. He stepped closer to her and reached up to push the jacket from her shoulders. It fell on the carpet of pine needles behind her. Slowly, Longarm unfastened the remaining buttons on the shirt and then drew it off of her as well, leaving her nude from the waist up. The little freckles that were dusted so appealingly across her breasts were scattered over the rest of her torso as well. Longarm lifted his hands and cupped her breasts, moving the firm mounds of creamy flesh in small circles. Molly closed her eyes as a look of sheer pleasure washed over her face.

Longarm squeezed her left breast and lowered his head to bring the nipple to his lips. He closed them gently over the brown nubbin and sucked lightly. Molly took his hat off so that she could let her fingers play through his thick dark hair as he suckled her. Little exhalations of joy came from her lips as gradually Longarm took more and more of her breast into his mouth. Finally he had almost all of it drawn in, and his tongue circled the nipple in wet swipes.

While he was doing that, he reached down with his other hand and unfastened her belt, then started working on the buttons of her denim trousers. They opened under his deft touch, and a moment later the pants slid down around her calves. She was wearing the bottom half of a pair of long underwear, and Longarm pushed that down as well. As he did, he abandoned her breast so that he could kneel in front of her as he lowered the barrier between himself and her womanhood. The triangle of finespun red hair came into view. It was long and silky and already sparkled in places with the dew of her rising passion. Molly gasped in surprise as Longarm buried his face in it.

She smelled clean and eager. As Longarm nuzzled her, he reached around and caught hold of her buttocks, squeezing and kneading them. Molly gasped again as he spread her cheeks apart and ran a fingertip lightly down the cleft between them. "Oh, Custis," she moaned softly. Her thighs spread instinctively.

Longarm rose in front of her, still cupping her bottom so that he lifted her into the air. She seemed light, almost like nothing in his arms. He bent and placed her carefully on the ground, laying her on the jacket and the shirt he had dropped behind her. He grasped her boots and pulled them off, and with a couple of kicks of her legs, she had shed the trousers and long underwear as well. She was naked before him now, her breath coming in sharp little pants from her parted lips.

Longarm liked to be undressed by a woman who took her time and knew what to do along the way, but both of them sensed that this wasn't the right time for such sensual languor. Their need was too urgent, too sharp-edged. He skinned out of his clothes as quickly as he could. Molly let out an excla-

144

mation of surprise and joy as he pushed down his trousers and his shaft bobbed into view. It was iron-hard and throbbing as Longarm dropped to his knees in front of her. He put his hands on her thighs and spread them. Unresisting, she opened herself to him. He moved over her, and she reached down to grasp him and guide him home.

With a thrust of his hips, Longarm entered her, sliding his shaft into the slick grip of her womanhood. She was incredibly tight, and he paused as she let out a small noise that could have been either pleasure or pain.

In a husky whisper, he asked, "Are you sure you've done this before, Molly?"

She clutched at his back, her fingernails digging into his flesh. "Oh, God, Custis, don't stop! Make love to me! Please make love to me!" She reached up and drew his head down to her, kissing him with all the passion and urgency in her body.

There was no turning back. Longarm drove ahead, feeling the momentary obstruction that barred his path give way under the onslaught of his burgeoning manhood. He was ready for Molly's reaction and clapped a hand over her mouth before her scream could rip out. She had lied to him about her past, and for the first time in he couldn't remember how long, he had just deflowered a virgin. Luckily, he hadn't completely forgotten what to do in a case like this. He held himself still, his shaft buried in her to the hilt, as the pain faded and the pleasure she was feeling began to grow. Only when her frenzied breathing had slowed a little did he take his hand away from her mouth.

"Are you all right?" he asked.

Wordlessly, she nodded. The way she was beginning to clutch at him again and move her hips back and forth was really all the answer he needed. He began sliding in and out of her in a steady rhythm that was as timeless as the stars.

Faster and faster, Longarm thrust into her. His breath rasped in his throat. He was glad they weren't any higher on the mountain. If the air had been any thinner, they might have both passed out. He felt his climax building, and Molly seemed to be nearing her culmination too. She gasped into his mouth as he kissed her, her breath warm and sweet.

Longarm thrust one last time, his great goad prodding deep into her feminine recesses, and stayed there as his climax shook him. Shuddering, he spurted into her, time after time. His arms pressed her tightly against him as his fluids gushed into her, filling her chamber and spilling out around his buried manhood. He worried again that she would scream, but instead she let her breath out in a long, quavery sigh. Every muscle in her body seemed to go limp as he gave one final spasm.

After a moment, Longarm rolled off her and flopped onto his back beside her. Both of them were still breathing hard. Molly rolled toward him, snuggling against his side and throwing a leg over his thighs. She pillowed her head on his shoulder.

Longarm lifted his head and looked down into her face. "You should have told me the truth," he said.

"Would you have done it if I had?"

"Well . . . I reckon I might not have."

She closed her eyes and rested her head against him again. "Don't worry, Custis. I'm not expecting anything from you other than what you just gave me. It was the most wonderful moment of my life, and it's plenty . . . for now."

"Meaning . . . ?"

"Meaning I know you have to move on when your job here is finished. I wouldn't ask you to stay, wouldn't expect you to. But now, when I settle down and get married, I'll know that whatever happens in the future, I've experienced the best lovemaking a woman could ever want."

Longarm didn't say anything. He figured she would find out soon enough that she was wrong. When she found the right man and decided to spend the rest of her life with him, it would be even better.

For now, he was content to lie there and enjoy her closeness. His fingertips played along her back and stroked the curve of her hip, then strayed back to the cleft of her bottom and toyed with it for a moment, long enough so that she was starting to breath harder again and rub her mound against his leg.

That was when they both heard the sound of a rider making his slow but steady way up the coulee toward the little high country valley.

Chapter 13

"Somebody's coming," said Longarm as he sat up sharply. Beside him, Molly gasped and rolled away from him, snatching up her clothes as she came to her feet.

Longarm was up too, pulling his pants on and stomping into his boots. He shrugged into his shirt but didn't bother buttoning it. Picking up his gunbelt and hat, he said to Molly, "Let's get behind these trees. Whoever that is, I'd just as soon he didn't see us."

Molly's face was red with embarrassment. "What if it's Joe?" she said. "Or my father?" Those words came out of her almost in a wail.

Under other circumstances, Longarm might have chuckled. It was nice to see that she wasn't quite the brazen hussy she liked to pretend she was, even after what they had just done. Now, though, he just caught hold of her arm and said, "Come on."

The trees here didn't grow densely enough to provide a hiding place, Longarm knew. He and Molly caught up the reins of their mounts and started toward the far end of the valley, moving quietly so that whoever was riding up the coulee wouldn't hear *them*. There was a jumble of large boulders there, and as Longarm and Molly led the horses among the rocks, they quickly lost sight of where they had been only a moment earlier. That was good, because it meant that whoever was coming wouldn't be able to see them either when he reached the valley.

Longarm handed his horse's reins to Molly and said, "Stay here." He turned back toward the valley.

"What are you going to do?" she asked.

"I want to find a place where I can get a look at that fella, whoever he is. Maybe he was trailing us, maybe he wasn't. If he wasn't, then he has to have some *other* reason for riding up into this high country."

Molly's eyes widened. "Maybe he's one of the men you're looking for."

"Could be," said Longarm. "That's what I'm going to find out." He paused and added, "I mean it, Molly. Stay here. You go to blundering around, you could get us both killed."

She nodded, her face pale. "I understand, Custis."

He hoped she truly did. Leaving her there, he made his way back through the nest of boulders and found a tiny crack between a couple of them where he could watch the valley without being observed in turn.

The sound of hoofbeats was louder now. Whoever the rider was, he wasn't taking any pains to be quiet. Almost as if he belonged here and didn't expect anyone to challenge him.

Longarm saw the horse's head first as the newcomer crossed the valley. Then the rider himself came into view. He wore lace-up work boots, thick canvas trousers, and a woolen shirt under a corduroy jacket. A flat-crowned black hat was on his head. Longarm got a good look at his hawk-like profile and bushy gray eyebrows.

Jared Flint.

"Son of a bitch!" Longarm breathed, hissing the words almost inaudibly through his teeth. He felt like kicking himself. As the foreman of Aurora's logging operation, Flint was in a perfect position to cause trouble for her. Longarm knew he should have seen that before now. He might have, he realized, had he not been distracted first by the hostility between the loggers and the cowboys of the Diamond K, then by Ben Callahan's words and actions, which couldn't have been any more suspicious if Callahan had set out to make Longarm think he was behind the trouble.

With a grimace, Longarm reined in his wildly galloping thoughts. Maybe he was jumping to conclusions yet again, he reminded himself. Flint might have some legitimate reason for being up here. Maybe he was scouting out the timber, seeing if it would be worthwhile for the McEntire Timber Company to extend their logging all the way to these upper slopes.

But that wasn't very likely, thought Longarm. An experienced man like Flint would know that this close to the timberline, it would be more trouble than the trees were worth to get them down to the sawmill. Longarm tried to think of some other reason for Flint to be here, but he couldn't come up with one.

Unless Flint was meeting with the killers he had hired to prod the loggers and the cattlemen into open warfare that would ultimately ruin both sides. Longarm didn't know what motive Flint might have for doing that, but it was looking more and more likely that that was exactly what had happened.

Longarm gave a little shake of his head. Flint had moved on out of Longarm's view by now. The lawman carefully edged around the boulder so that he could peer after the rider. Flint had crossed the valley and was climbing still higher now, taking a trail so faint that Longarm could barely see it. Longarm turned and hurried back to where he had left Molly and the horses.

"Who was it?" she asked anxiously when he reached her hiding place among the boulders.

"Nobody you know," Longarm told her. "A fella named Jared Flint. He's the foreman of the McEntire logging operation."

She looked confused. "What would someone like that be doing up here? There's not enough trees this high up to make it worthwhile for the loggers to cut them down."

Not only beautiful but smart too, thought Longarm. Molly was reaching the same conclusion he had, following the same

149

line of logic. He saw awareness dawn in her eyes as she looked at him.

"Custis, he could be the one behind all the trouble!" she exclaimed.

Longarm nodded. "Yep. That's why I'm going to follow him. If those hired guns are hiding up here, Flint must be on his way to meet with them, maybe give them a new job."

"What are you going to do?"

"Follow him, try to find out just what he's up to."

Molly reached for her horse's reins. "I'm ready. Let's go."

Longarm caught hold of her arm and stopped her. "Not hardly," he said. "You're going back down the mountain—now."

"No, I'm not," Molly said defiantly. "I'm going to help you."

"That's what I meant. Go back to the ranch and tell your pa and Joe Traywick what's going on up here. Tell 'em to send some of the Diamond K hands up that coulee, and have 'em be ready for trouble. I'm liable to need reinforcements, Molly."

She looked doubtful. "I don't know . . ."

"It's the best thing you can do for me," he told her honestly.

"Well . . . all right." Her agreement was reluctant, but Longarm hoped she would go through with it.

"I just wouldn't mention anything else that happened up here," he added, pulling the sheepskin jacket closed over her torn shirt and buttoning it. He was aware of the soft pressure of her breasts against the cloth, but tried not to think about what had gone on earlier. He didn't need that sort of distraction right now.

"Don't worry," she said. "That was just between the two of us." She came up on her toes and kissed him again, hard. "And I'll never forget it, Custis. Never."

"Neither will I," he told her, knowing that was what she wanted to hear. Knowing too that there was a grain of truth in what he said. The memory might fade, but it would always be there, deep inside him. He turned her around and patted her on the rump. "Now scoot."

150

She mounted up and walked her horse out of the boulders. Longarm followed. Both of them moved carefully and quietly. The grass in the tiny valley helped muffle the steps of the horses. When they reached the upper end of the coulee, Molly paused and turned to give Longarm a brave smile. He smiled and nodded, then waved her into motion once more. She started down the coulee.

He turned and rode across the valley to the spot where the upper trail began, the trail that Jared Flint had taken. It was little more than a goat path. Longarm knew he was going to have to be very careful. The vegetation up here was sparse, so there was little cover. If Flint looked back at the wrong time, he was liable to spot Longarm following him.

That was a chance he was going to have to take, Longarm told himself. Fortunately, the trail had a lot of twists and bends in it as it weaved up toward the peak, and there were more of those good-sized boulders scattered about, providing a few hiding places if necessary. His nerves taut with anticipation, Longarm began climbing once more.

Once again, he was thankful for the good fortune that had led him to rent such a trustworthy mount from the livery stable in Timber City. The roan never faltered as it made its way up the steep slope. It placed each hoof carefully, so that no stones rolled underneath its feet. Such a slip could have led to a bad fall; at best, the clatter of rocks bouncing down the mountain might alert Flint that someone was following him. But with the help of the roan, Longarm was able to proceed steadily up the slope. Every so often, he caught a glimpse of Flint several hundred yards above him. When that happened, he slowed down a little, dropping back so that Flint couldn't see him should the timber company foreman happen to glance behind him.

The two men continued up the mountain, and Longarm had to wonder just how high Flint intended to go. Those stolen cattle couldn't have been driven this far up the peak, he decided. They had been disposed of in some other fashion, maybe taken through a pass to the other side of the Cascades. Either that, or they had been driven in the opposite direction, into the ranchlands of the broad Willamette Valley. Getting

151

rid of them there might have attracted more notice and raised more questions, but it wasn't inconceivable.

Maybe his whole theory was wrong, thought Longarm. Maybe there *wasn't* a hideout up here after all.

That was when he caught sight of a tendril of almost colorless smoke curling into the sky from somewhere several hundred yards above him. From the lower slopes of the mountain, the smoke would have been practically invisible.

Longarm grinned. Somebody had a campfire burning up here, and he figured that camp was Jared Flint's destination.

Longarm dismounted. Despite the roan's surefootedness, he would have to go the rest of the way on foot. Couldn't risk letting whoever was up there know that Flint had been followed. The wind had gotten stronger and chillier the higher Longarm climbed, so before he left the horse he took his jacket from the saddlebags and put it on.

"Sorry there's no graze for you here, old son," he said quietly as he patted the horse on the neck. "We'll be back down in grass country after a while."

He left the roan tied to a scrubby pine and started up the trail once more. His hand hovered near the butt of his Colt as he climbed. His heart was slugging heavily in his chest from the elevation, the exertion, and maybe a little bit from anticipation. He didn't know for sure what he was going to find, but he sensed he was drawing near the end of this case—one way or the other.

This high up the mountain, he thought it unlikely there would be any guards posted, but he kept his eyes and ears wide open just in case. He hadn't seen any sign of Flint for several minutes now.

Suddenly, a bench opened up in front of him. This shelf of fairly level land was several hundred yards long and half that deep. Longarm dropped into a crouch behind a boulder that was perched next to the rim. From there, he could see that the bench was much like the valley down below where he and Molly had made love, only somewhat larger. The ground had a thin cover of grass on it, and a few trees were clustered around what was evidently a spring of some sort. A little creek meandered off to the right end of the bench, where it spilled over the side in a waterfall. Longarm was willing to bet that water was mighty clear and mighty cold. It made him thirsty just thinking about it.

But his attention was focused much more on the trio of ramshackle cabins built around the spring. Old prospectors' shacks, more than likely, he thought, left over from the days when folks had hoped to find gold up here. Somebody had repaired the cabins and built a pole corral, in which a couple of dozen horses grazed.

The horse Jared Flint had been riding was tied up in front of one of the cabins. There was no other sign of the timber company foreman.

Flint had to be inside the cabin, thought Longarm, no doubt conferring with the men who were hiding out here. The men he had hired to raid the lumber camp, to rustle cattle from the Diamond K . . . and who knows what other deadly errands he had planned for them to carry out?

He had to get closer, Longarm knew. Had to find out just what the next step in Flint's scheme was going to be. He hoped that Molly had reached the ranch without any trouble, because he was going to need help rousting these outlaws from their den.

A foot scraped on rock behind him.

Longarm twisted, his hand flashing to the Colt on his hip. He palmed the gun from the cross-draw rig and started to bring it up, his finger tightening on the trigger. He expected the crash of a shot or the impact of a blow at any instant, and he cursed himself for getting so caught up in his thoughts that he had let someone sneak up on him. Such carelessness was probably about to be the death of him, but at least he would go down fighting.

He froze, finger taut on the trigger, as Molly stepped back sharply and gasped in fear and surprise.

"Son of a bitch!" Longarm hissed. "Girl, I almost blew your head off!" Tremors of reaction went through him.

"I . . . I didn't mean to startle you," Molly stammered. "I saw you up here, and I knew you must have . . . must have found something."

"Damn it, I sent you back down the mountain!"

"I . . . I decided to follow you. I was afraid you'd get in trouble—"

"Oh, I'm in trouble, all right," grated Longarm. "I've got a nest full of killers sitting right in front of me and no help on the way thanks to you."

Molly's features grew tight with anger. "All I wanted to do was help!"

The conversation was being carried on in whispers. Longarm wasn't worried that their words would carry to the hardcases he was sure were in those cabins conferring with Jared Flint. He *was* worried, though, that he and Molly might be spotted if there were any sentries posted around the hideout. He had planned to stay there, keeping an eye on the place until help arrived from the Diamond K.

But now he knew that no help was coming. The only thing he and Molly could do was slip away as quietly as possible and return to the ranch. With luck, maybe he could still thwart whatever Flint was planning to do next.

He took hold of Molly's arm. "Come on, we've got to get back down the mountain—"

"Freeze, mister!"

The shout came from Longarm's left. He twisted in that direction, the Colt he had drawn a moment earlier still in his hand. He pulled Molly behind him, prepared to shield her body with his own. His eyes spotted the man crouched behind a rock, the rifle in his hands trained on the two of them.

"Drop that gun, you bastard!"

That yell came from the other direction, and Longarm felt his heart sinking. They were trapped in a cross fire. He might have been able to swap lead with one man and come out of the exchange alive; two men with rifles, one to each side of him, meant that he and Molly would both die if any shooting broke out. He turned his head to glance over his shoulder, and saw the second guard covering him with a Winchester from about thirty yards away. Longarm wasn't sure where either of them had been hiding until now, but that didn't really matter. What was important was that he had been spotted while he was trailing Jared Flint up here.

"Take it easy on those triggers, gents," he called out to the

154

two outlaws as he lifted both hands, the Colt still in his right.

"Put the gun on the ground," yelled one of the men. Longarm complied with the order, bending to carefully place the Colt at his feet.

The other guard said, "Move away from it." He came out from behind the rock that had sheltered him and advanced toward Longarm and Molly, keeping the rifle trained on them. Behind him, Longarm heard the second guard approaching too. Longarm took several steps away from the Colt, and Molly moved with him.

"Custis . . ." she said, fear in her voice. Her arm was against his, and he could feel her trembling.

"Don't you worry," he said quietly. "We'll get out of this somehow."

He hoped he sounded more confident than he felt.

"Shit, I know you," said the guard in front of them as he came closer. "You're that U.S. marshal we tried to bushwhack a couple of times." The hired killer's lips pulled back from his teeth in an ugly grimace. "You killed a couple of friends of mine, Marshal."

"They were aiming to kill me," Longarm pointed out. "I didn't have much choice."

The second man came up behind them and laughed harshly at Longarm's comment. "Sure you did," he said. "You could've just gone ahead and died and saved us all a lot of trouble."

The first guard jerked the barrel of his Winchester toward the cabins. "Come on. We'll let Flint decide what to do with the two of you . . . though I reckon I've got a pretty good idea what he's going to say."

"Me too," the second man put in. "I figure we're goin' to kill you, mister—and then this pretty little gal's goin' to entertain us for a while."

More than ever, Longarm wished that Molly had gone on down the mountain like he'd told her to. Now there was nothing he could do for her, for either of them, except wait and watch for an opportunity to make a desperate bid for freedom.

Maybe if nothing else, they would die quickly that way.

They walked ahead of the two guards across the bench toward the spring and the cabins. When they were about fifty yards away, one of the outlaws lifted his voice and shouted "Hey, Boss, come out here and see what we found!"

The door of the largest cabin opened, and several hardcases emerged, followed by Jared Flint. The timber man stopped short when he saw Longarm. "Damn you, Long!" he exclaimed. "You just had to keep poking around, didn't you?"

"It's my job," Longarm said coolly as he came to a stop in front of Flint and the gunmen.

"So I suppose you're proud of yourself now. Finally found out what you wanted to know, didn't you?"

Longarm nodded. "I reckon so. You and these fellas you hired have been behind the trouble down below all the time, haven't you?"

"Of course. That government timber contract's going to make us all rich once I'm running things."

"You're already Mrs. McEntire's foreman. What more do you want?"

Flint snorted in contempt. "Angus McEntire was supposed to leave *me* in charge of the company when he died. I never dreamed that . . . that woman would come in and start trying to run things."

"Rubbed you the wrong way, did it, taking orders from a woman? Especially since she had the company doing so well?"

"It would have done even better with me in charge," said Flint. "And without Mrs. McEntire around, there wouldn't be anybody to stop me from taking all the profits. That's just what I'll do once she finally realizes she's not cut out for life in a lumber camp."

Longarm's eyes narrowed. He had run up against his share of grandiose criminal schemes in his time, some of which could have had pretty far-reaching implications for the entire country. Not this case, though. At the heart of it was nothing more than a venal, greedy embezzler—albeit on a fairly large scale, if Flint had his way.

"If that's all you wanted," said Longarm, "why didn't you just kill her and be done with it?"

Flint shook his head. "There are some things I won't do,

Marshal. I wasn't above arranging an accident so that Angus McEntire would die, but I'm not going to murder a woman in cold blood. Besides, that still wouldn't necessarily leave me in charge of the operation. I want Mrs. McEntire alive and trusting me—at least until I get my hands on enough loot to make it all worthwhile.''

One of the gunmen said, ''That's enough jabberin'. Let's kill this badge-totin' skunk and be done with it.'' He leered. ''I want to make the acquaintance o' that gal with him anyway.''

''Shut up, Barcroft.'' Flint turned to Molly. ''You're Molly Kinsman, aren't you?'' he demanded.

She managed to nod, and her chin trembled only slightly as she did so. For the moment, she was holding on to her self-control with an iron grip, Longarm thought, but sooner or later that grip was going to weaken.

''Sorry you got mixed up in this, Miss Kinsman,'' said Flint, and he sounded as if he meant it. ''Wish there was some way around what's going to have to happen, but I don't reckon there is.''

Longarm knew he'd be wasting his breath if he pleaded for Molly's life. Now that she knew Flint was the mastermind, she would have to die too, though Longarm had no doubt the hired killers would keep her alive for a while before disposing of her. It wouldn't be a reprieve for her. They would take turns assaulting her until she was more dead than alive.

Flint turned to the burly gunman called Barcroft, who seemed to be the leader of these hired gunmen. ''We'd better get moving,'' he said. ''Get that dynamite loaded. I want to reach the dam just after dark.''

Barcroft nodded, but instead of following Flint's orders, he jerked a thumb at Longarm and Molly. ''What about them?''

''There'll be plenty of time to deal with them later. Put them in one of the cabins and leave a couple of men to guard them.''

''Likely be better to kill the lawman now,'' said Barcroft, fingering the butt of his gun.

Flint shook his head firmly. ''Not yet. I want Long to see some of what's in store for Miss Kinsman before he dies.''

Longarm's jaw tightened. So Flint wasn't just an ambitious

crook. He had a cruel streak in him too, a streak of pure meanness.

But that was all right, Longarm told himself. As long as he was still drawing breath, there was a chance for him and Molly to get out of this. Mighty slim, to be sure, but a chance nonetheless.

Whatever hopes Longarm had were quickly stifled. He and Molly were trussed up and shoved into one of the shacks, and Longarm knew without struggling against his bonds that their captors had done a professional job of tying them up. He might be able to work enough slack into the rope to worm his hands free—with a considerable loss of blood and hide in the process—but it would take too long. The outlaws who were preparing to leave the hidden camp planned to return before the coming night was over. Then they would have their fun with Molly and kill Longarm.

In the dimness of the shack, Longarm could see the pale blur that was Molly's face. "I really ruined things, didn't I?" she said miserably.

"Nope," Longarm told her. "Those fellas would have jumped me anyway. I knew I was walking into a lion's den right from the start, Molly. That's why I didn't want you along."

"But if I'd gone for help like you told me . . ."

Longarm sighed. There was no denying that their situation would look at least a little brighter right now if they had hopes of a bunch of Diamond K cowboys riding to their rescue. Unfortunately, it wasn't going to happen.

Molly had fallen silent, overwhelmed by the predicament in which they found themselves. They heard the sound of a lot of horses leaving the camp, and Longarm knew Flint, Barcroft, and the other gunnies had set out on their latest mission of destruction. After a few minutes, Molly said, "What was that Flint said about dynamite? And a dam?"

"I've been thinking about that too," replied Longarm. "The loggers built a dam on one of the upper creeks so that a pond would back up and give them enough water to run a flume down the mountain to the sawmill. I reckon Flint's going to blow it to kindling."

"A flume?" repeated Molly. "What's that?"

Longarm searched his mind for a way to explain the apparatus. "It's sort of like a creek on stilts," he said after a minute. "It's a big trough lined with pitch so it's watertight, set up on poles so that it runs in an elevated line down the mountain. The loggers let water into it through a sluice gate in the dam on a lake or a pond, and of course the water runs downhill. If you roll a log into the flume, it floats down too. It's a quicker, easier way to move the logs than hauling them out with mules or a donkey engine and cables. Timber companies use it when there's no stream nearby that's big enough to float booms of logs."

"Well, I'll take your word for it," said Molly, trying to inject a note of lightness into her voice despite their situation. "I was raised on a cattle ranch, and none of this logging business really makes sense to me. But if Mrs. McEntire's men built that dam, why would Flint want to blow it up?"

"That much water, turned loose all of a sudden like that, will flood the logging camp and maybe drown some of the men. Maybe Flint's hoping that'll be the last straw for Mrs. McEntire. All he really wants to do is run her off without hurting the operation too much. Of course, he don't seem to care how many men he kills along the way."

"He's a horrible man," Molly said with a shudder.

"Yep," agreed Longarm. "That he is."

"And . . . and . . . he's going to kill us. . . ." Molly's voice began to quaver, and Longarm could tell that her self-imposed calm was about to shatter.

He was trying to come up with something to tell her when he heard one of the guards who had been left outside the cabin say abruptly, "Hey, who's that old man? Hold it right there, mister! What're you doin' up here?"

Another of the guards said scornfully, "Aw, take it easy, Jed. It's just an old Chinaman. Prob'ly a peddler."

"On top of a mountain? Not damn likely." Longarm heard the lever of a Winchester being worked. "I said stop, mister. What do you want?"

Longarm had felt his pulse jump when he heard the word "Chinaman," and now his hopes rose even more as a familiar voice said, "No pointee gun, please. Mist' Flint send me, tell you hurry down mountain. Much trouble below."

Wing. That was Wing out there, Longarm realized.

"What'n hell? Why would Flint send you with a message for us? I ain't never even seen you before, Chinaman."

"This humble one is cook in logging camp," Wing lied. "Helpee Mist' Flint much times before."

"Well . . . I don't know. I still ain't sure we ought to trust you. What do you think, Pete?"

The other guard was about to say something when Longarm heard a meaty thunk. Somebody yelled, "Son of a—," but then the startled shout died away in a hideous gurgle. Inside the cabin, Longarm and Molly looked at each other, wide-eyed with hope and surprise.

The door opened and Wing stepped inside, shaking his head so that his queue swung back and forth. He looked down at Longarm and Molly and said, "Missy Molly ver' naughty girl. Lucky old Chinese man follow in case she get in trouble."

"Oh, hell, Wing, stop talking like that and get these ropes off us," Longarm said urgently. "Are those guards dead?"

Wing nodded. "Yep, both of 'em. Are they the only ones Flint left behind?" He knelt beside Longarm and began using the knife he held in his hand to saw at the ropes binding the lawman's wrists. Longarm noticed that the slender blade was stained with blood.

"As far as I know," Longarm said. "I think all the others went with Flint to blow up a dam on a creek down the mountain." He grunted in satisfaction as the ropes came free. While Wing moved to his legs to cut those bonds, Longarm began rubbing the circulation back into his hands.

"Wing, what are you doing here?" asked Molly in amazement.

Wing finished freeing Longarm's legs and moved over to start on Molly's bonds. "As soon as Joe told me what he had told you," he said, "I knew you'd be following old Custis here. So *I* followed *you.*"

"You came up that coulee on the side of the mountain?" asked Longarm.

"Yeah, but somebody was ahead of me. That fella Flint. I

recognized him from that time the loggers attacked the ranch. You and him and that Miz McEntire came riding up in time to keep anybody from getting hurt too bad.''

"Flint led us on a so-called shortcut that day," Longarm said bitterly. "I figure he was really delaying us in hopes we'd be too late to stop a full-scale battle from breaking out. Luckily he didn't slow us down quite enough."

"You . . . you followed me," said Molly, still stuck on that point. Longarm wondered if she was worried that the Chinese cook had seen the two of them making love. Now that they weren't both about to die, she could spare some concern for something like that. Longarm didn't care overmuch, but he was pretty sure Wing knew nothing about that part of the afternoon. Wing had come up the coulee behind Flint, and by that time, Molly's deflowering had long since been accomplished. If Molly had gone on down the mountain as Longarm had told her to, in fact, doubtless she would have run right into Wing on his way up.

"That coulee was a busy place with folks coming and going today," Longarm commented as Wing helped Molly to her feet. "Now we've all got to get down the mountain again, as fast as we can. Maybe we can still stop Flint."

Wing slid a finger along the edge of his blade. "I'd like that," he said, and Molly stared at him, as if seeing him for the first time.

She was even more surprised and horrified a moment later when the three of them stepped out of the cabin and she saw the bodies sprawled face-down on the ground. One of the outlaws had a hatchet buried in the back of his head while the other was lying in a pool of rapidly drying blood that had gushed from his slit throat. Longarm looked at the corpses too, and said to Wing, "I reckon in your earlier days, you must've done a little work for some of those tongs down in San Francisco."

"Tongs?" repeated Wing, his face and voice emotionless. "This humble one is but a cook."

Longarm grinned tiredly and shook his head, knowing there was no point in carrying on with this conversation. No matter what Wing had been in the past, he was a good friend now.

161

Hell, he had saved their lives, pure and simple, and he was going to help Longarm put an end to Jared Flint's schemes too.

Flint was going to be one surprised son of a bitch the next time he saw Longarm.

And Longarm hoped fervently that next time was going to be over the barrel of a gun.

Chapter 14

The horses ridden up there by Longarm and Molly had been brought up to the camp from where they had been left and put into the corral. Wing retrieved the mounts while Longarm helped himself to a six-gun and some extra shells from one of the dead guards. Then the three of them started back down the mountain.

At the bottom of the coulee, they split up, over Molly's objections. Longarm sent her to the Diamond K with orders to bring as many men as possible to the headquarters of the McEntire timber operation. "Your pa might not believe me if I told him what's going on," said Longarm, "but I'm betting he'll believe you."

"I'll make sure of it," she promised grimly.

Longarm turned to the cook. "Wing, you head for the logging camp and warn them about what Flint's planning to do. Maybe if they know a flood's on the way, they can avoid the worst of it. Once the punchers from the Diamond K get there, bring them and Mrs. McEntire's men up the mountain to that dam. Even if I can slow down Flint and his men and keep them from blowing up the dam, I'm liable to need a hand by then.''

"You can't stop them by yourself," protested Molly. "There are too many of them!"

Longarm grinned. "Reckon I'll just have to make do. Now git, both of you!''

Reluctantly, Wing and Molly galloped away on different trails. Longarm took yet a third path, sending the roan down a narrow trail that he hoped would take him where he needed to go.

He had only a vague idea of where the dam was located, and he didn't have a lot of time to spend searching. A glance at the sky told him that the sun was lowering toward the peaks of the Cascade range. Flint had said he wanted to reach the dam just after dark. That was a good time for the explosion he had planned. None of the loggers would be there, because they would all be down in the main camp, sitting down to supper. The torrent of water that would race down the mountainside following the blast would take them completely by surprise unless Wing got there in time to alert them to their danger. They might have a little warning, Longarm corrected himself, because they might hear the explosion that destroyed the dam. But that would be too little, too late, especially since the loggers would have no way of knowing what had caused the blast.

There was a lot riding on him, Longarm realized—not only justice for a clever criminal, but also the lives of innocent men.

And possibly the life of Aurora McEntire as well.

Despite Flint's high-flown statements about not wanting to kill Aurora, he had come close before, when he or one of his henchmen had set free that boom to come crashing into Aurora's cabin. The flood that would wash down the mountain after the dam was destroyed wouldn't differentiate between its victims either. As long as she was in the camp, Aurora was in deadly danger.

As shadows gathered, Longarm had to watch the trail closely. From landmarks on the mountain and in the valleys below, he estimated that he was almost directly above the timber camp now, which meant he should be reaching the dam soon. Despite the fact that any delay chafed at him, he slowed the roan to a walk so that the pounding of its hoofbeats wouldn't advertise that he was coming. If he was going to have any chance to stop Flint's plan, he had to take the men at the dam by surprise.

Suddenly, he heard voices, and he reined the horse to a quick stop. He swung down from the saddle and tied the roan to a nearby bush. "Stay here, old son," he whispered to the horse as he patted it on the neck. Then he started on foot along the path, which had all but disappeared in the thickening dusk.

Through a screen of brush and trees, he saw the dam looming ahead of him. It was built of logs, naturally enough, and had a sluice gate in its center, several feet below the top of the dam. A surefooted logger could walk out there on the dam, bend over and grasp a handle, and pull the gate up to release the water into the flume, which was already partially built. Longarm's gaze followed the steeply inclined, elevated trough as it ran down the mountainside and disappeared into the shadows. He didn't know how much of the flume had been completed, but if that dynamite went off as Flint planned, it would be destroyed along with the dam.

The flume and the dam itself could be rebuilt, though, once Flint had succeeded in running off Aurora McEntire. After all, the money wouldn't be coming out of his pocket.

Longarm crouched behind the thick trunk of a pine and searched the dam and the area around it for any sign of Flint and the man's hired gunmen. Surely he hadn't beaten them to the punch and gotten there first. That wasn't possible.

Nor was it the case, Longarm saw a moment later. A couple of men emerged from the shadows on the far side of the dam and began walking carefully out onto the wall of logs. No doubt the rest of the gang were over there too, in the trees beyond the big pond that had been formed by the dam. Stars were beginning to twinkle into existence in the darkening sky above, and Longarm could see the pinpoints of light reflected in the calm surface of the pond. "Lake" would have been a better word to describe the recently formed body of water, he thought; it was already larger than any pond he had ever seen. The surroundings reminded him a little of Lake Tahoe, down in Nevada, where a couple of cases had taken him in the past.

In the gloom, Longarm couldn't see the two men on the dam that well, but he thought they were Flint and Barcroft. They had just about reached the center of the dam. Longarm edged closer, using the brush for cover, and saw one of the men strike a match. The sudden glare of the lucifer revealed the craggy features of Jared Flint. Flint extended the match toward the other man, who was indeed Barcroft, Longarm confirmed. Barcroft held several sticks of dynamite that had been tied together. A single long fuse ran from the deadly bundle.

"I'll light it," said Flint, "and you wedge it down there behind that sluice gate lever."

Barcroft nodded. "All right, but don't waste any time gettin' off of here once the fuse is lit. It ought to burn for several minutes, but you can't never be sure about such things."

Longarm drew his gun as Flint held the match to the fuse. It caught with a sharp, serpent-like hissing sound. Barcroft knelt to place the dynamite.

Longarm knew he couldn't wait for them to leave the dam, then run out there himself and pull the fuse. That would be cutting it too fine. He did the only thing he could.

He shot Barcroft.

It was getting too dark for any fancy marksmanship. Longarm aimed for the gunman's bulky body and squeezed the trigger. As the Colt bucked against his palm, Barcroft let out a howl of pain and flew backwards, driven off the dam by the impact of the slug. He fell into the waters of the pond with a huge splash, the dynamite going with him just as Longarm had hoped it would. The water put out the fuse and rendered the explosives harmless.

Flint twisted toward the sound of the shot and yelled a curse. He brought up a gun and blazed away at the spot where Longarm crouched. Longarm threw himself flat as bullets whipped through the brush above him.

"Somebody's over there!" shouted Flint to his men. "Get him! Get the son of a bitch!"

More yelling came from the rest of the gunmen. Some of them started shooting across the water, their muzzle flashes winking like giant fireflies in the dusk, while others began running around the pond in an effort to close in on Longarm.

Meanwhile, Flint turned and dashed off the dam with the ease of a man who had spent quite a bit of time on such structures in the past.

Longarm thought bleakly that the foreman was probably going back for more dynamite.

On his hands and knees, Longarm crawled rapidly toward the dam. He didn't want to shoot at Flint's men because his own muzzle flashes would just give them something at which to aim. When he had almost reached the dam, he slid down the steep slope and wound up in the thick shadows underneath the flume.

Longarm moved under the flume in a crouching run and came out on the other side. Craning his neck, he looked up at the top of the dam looming above him. As he had feared, Flint was starting out onto the dam once more. Longarm was convinced he had brought more dynamite with him.

The hired killers were still throwing lead into the place where Longarm had been a few minutes earlier, but they weren't hitting anything except some tree branches. Longarm knew it wouldn't take them long to realize he had gotten out of there once some of the gunmen reached the far side of the pond. He went to one of the thick logs that supported the framework of the flume and wrapped his arms and legs around it. He began shinnying up the pole toward the flume itself.

As he climbed, he heard the sudden pounding of hoofbeats in the forest nearby. Someone yelled, "Over there!" Longarm thought it might have been Matt Kinsman. A moment later, more guns began to bang. The dusk was lit by near-constant flashes of exploding gunpowder.

The help he had sent Molly and Wing for had arrived—and just in time too.

Longarm kept climbing. He leaned his head back and looked up, spotting the dark figure of Jared Flint atop the dam. Flint was fumbling with something, and it didn't take a genius to figure out what it was. Longarm lost sight of the man as he reached the flume itself. He reached up and caught hold of the trough's edge with one hand, then two. Pain shrieked in his back as he pushed off from the framework with his legs and dangled there for a moment. That bullet crease was not yet fully healed, and Longarm figured he had just torn it open again.

He pushed the pain away to be dealt with later. Pulling himself up with a grunt of effort, he swung a leg over the flume's edge and caught his heel on it. He was able to lever himself up and roll over, landing in the still-dry flume. The angle was extreme, but he began scrambling toward the top, even as Flint struck another match and moved it toward the fuse of the second bundle of dynamite.

"Flint!" Longarm bellowed, trying to startle the man into dropping the match or the dynamite or both. Instead, Flint jerked his head around to peer down into the flume, and in the light of the match, his features contorted with hate as he saw Longarm climbing toward him. With a sneer, he reached down for the sluice gate handle with the hand holding the match.

Longarm's eyes widened, and he threw all of his strength into lunging upward toward Flint. There was no time for gunplay now, only for a desperate grab. Longarm's hand shot out and closed over Flint's ankle just as the timber company foreman pulled the sluice gate.

Water slammed into Longarm and rocketed him back down the flume, but his fingers were still wrapped around Flint's ankle in a grip of iron. With a yell, Flint was jerked off the dam and crashed down into the flume just above Longarm. The force of the water carried both of them down the mountainside in a mad, careening ride.

Longarm's mouth was full of water. He spit out as much of it as he could and coughed up some more. The racing water, which was moving with enough force to carry huge logs down the flume, slammed him into the sides of the structure. He bounced off and kept going. He had ridden the rapids of some raging rivers in his time, and this experience was somewhat similar. There was nothing he could do except let himself go limp and hope the wild ride wouldn't kill him.

Something hit him in the head, but it wasn't the side of the flume. It was Jared Flint's work-booted foot. Flint kicked at Longarm again as he slid down alongside the lawman. The flume was wide enough for both of them to go flying down it side by side. Through the turbulent water that splashed in his face, Longarm saw Flint reaching for him, felt the man's fingers close around his throat.

Longarm was already gasping for breath due to the fact that his head was constantly going in and out of the water. Flint had caught him at a bad time, when there was little air in his lungs. Desperate, Longarm struck out at Flint with his fists, hoping to knock Flint's grip loose. Instead the fingers only tightened. A gray haze that had nothing to do with nightfall began settling over Longarm's vision. He knew he was very close to losing consciousness, and if he did, Flint would kill him.

Then, suddenly, there was nothing underneath him. The water fell away, leaving Longarm and Flint shooting through thin air.

Of course, thought Longarm. The construction of the flume had only started.

They had reached the end of the line.

Instinctively, Longarm grasped Flint's shirt and twisted in midair as they traveled through a long, graceful curve toward the ground. Tree branches caught at them, slowing them slightly, then with a crash that jolted all of Longarm's teeth, they slammed into the earth. Longarm's quick thinking had put Flint on the bottom, though, and he bore the brunt of the impact. Flint's fingers were torn from Longarm's throat as their landing knocked the two men apart and sent them rolling separately down the slope.

Water was gushing in rivulets around Longarm when he finally came to a stop. The torrent pouring off the end of the flume was washing down the mountainside. The cold water revived the stunned lawman, and he lifted his head to look toward the flume. As he watched, the flood came to a halt, dying away to a trickle. Someone up above had thought to lower the sluice gate once more. There were no more shots coming from up there either. The fight was over.

Longarm wondered who had won.

For the time being, he was more concerned with Jared Flint. Here under the trees, the shadows were even thicker and darker, but after a moment he spotted the sprawled bulk that could only be Flint. Longarm pushed himself to his feet, groaning at the pain shooting through his battered body. He stumbled toward Flint, and as he did, he checked the holster on his hip. The gun he had taken from the dead guard at the outlaw camp was gone, which came as no surprise.

He didn't need it, he told himself. If Flint put up a fight, Longarm would kill the son of a bitch with his bare hands.

Flint wasn't going to be putting up a fight, though, not ever again. Longarm dropped to one knee beside the man, who lay on his back staring up sightlessly at the stars now appearing through the spaces in the canopy of trees. Slamming into the ground at such high speed with Longarm on top of him like that had probably busted up Flint inside. When Longarm grasped Flint's shoulder and turned him onto his side, even in the faint starlight he could see that the damage was much worse. The whole back of Flint's skull was caved in. He had to have died almost instantly.

With a sigh, Longarm pushed himself to his feet. The threat of Flint's schemes was over. Now he had to hope that Flint's hired gunmen had been dealt with as well.

"Custis! Damn it, Custis, where are you?"

Longarm lifted his head. That was Molly Kinsman's voice. She wouldn't be up here unless the forces led by her father had won the battle. Longarm began trudging wearily up the mountainside toward the dam.

When he reached it a few minutes later, looking no doubt like a half-drowned rat, he saw that several lanterns had been lit. Matt Kinsman's cowboys and some of the loggers from Aurora's camp were standing together around several prisoners, covering the captured gunmen with rifles. Molly, Matt Kinsman, Joe Traywick, Wing, Aurora McEntire, and Ben Callahan, of all people, stood near the dam. Molly spotted Longarm and ran toward him, shouting excitedly, "Custis!" She threw her arms around him, ignoring his soaked clothing.

Kinsman strode after her, followed by Traywick, who limped along being supported by Wing. Traywick's injured foot hadn't stopped him from being in on this showdown.

Aurora and Callahan joined the group clustering around Longarm.

"You all right, Marshal?" Kinsman demanded gruffly. "Or is my daughter about to squeeze you to death?"

"I reckon . . . I'll be fine once I catch my breath," said Longarm. Actually, every muscle and bone in his body ached, and the old wound on his back hurt like blazes. He was going to need some time to recuperate from this job.

Kinsman jerked a thumb at the prisoners. "We rounded up this bunch, them that didn't make us kill 'em. Found one floatin' in the pond too. Reckon that was probably your doin'."

Barcroft, thought Longarm. He nodded wearily. Molly wasn't hugging him anymore, but she still had an arm around him as she stood beside him. Longarm looked at Kinsman and then at Aurora and said, "Glad to see that you two finally decided you could work together."

"Once this Chinese gentleman showed up at the camp and told us what you'd found out, there wasn't much choice," said Aurora.

"When I first got to this part of the country," Longarm pointed out, "you never would've believed him since he works for Kinsman."

"Well . . . I hope that such distrust is behind us now." Aurora looked at Kinsman.

"Far as I'm concerned it is," the rancher grunted. "I still ain't overly fond of what you've been doin' up here, but I'll make an effort to get along if you will, ma'am."

Aurora stuck out her hand toward him. "Of course."

Kinsman took her hand, and they shook on it. Longarm felt a surge of satisfaction that gave him some renewed energy. One of the things he had set out to do had been accomplished. With luck, there would be peace between the cattlemen and the loggers from here on out.

He looked at Callahan and asked, "What are you doing up here?"

"I was at Aurora's camp," Callahan said rather awkwardly, "explaining myself to her."

"Asking me to marry him, he means," Aurora said, with a

laugh. "You could have knocked me over with a feather, Ben. I always thought you couldn't stand me."

"I hope you know now that's not true."

"Certainly I do." She linked her arm with his. "And I'm very tempted to take you up on your offer to merge our companies."

"I don't think that's all he wants to merge," Molly blurted out.

Kinsman glared at her, but the others all laughed. After a moment, even the rancher gave a rueful chuckle. He said, "We'd better gather up those prisoners and all the bodies and cart 'em into town. Deputy Bullfinch'll have to make room in his jail for the live ones."

"Plenty of room at the undertaker's for the dead ones," Joe Traywick put in.

Aurora stepped closer to Longarm. "Custis, where is Mr. Flint?"

Longarm inclined his head down the mountainside. "Back yonder at the end of that flume. Both of us went shooting off there, but Flint hit headfirst." Longarm shook his head. "He won't be causing any more trouble unless he's already trying to take over from the Devil down there in Hades."

Tugging gently on his arm, Molly led Longarm away. "I'm going to take good care of you," she said. "We'll have you back on your feet in no time."

"Sounds good to me," said Longarm.

"And then we'll have you on your back."

He looked over at her quizzically.

"*I* want to be on top next time," she whispered.

SPECIAL PREVIEW

They were the most brutal gang of cutthroats ever
assembled. And during the Civil War, they sought
justice outside of the law. Paying back every Yankee
raid with one of their own. They rode hard, shot
straight, and had their way with every willing woman
west of the Mississippi. No man could stop them. No
woman could resist them. And no Yankee stood a
chance of living when Quantrill's Raiders rode into
town . . .

BUSHWHACKERS
by B. J. Lanagan

Coming July 1997 in paperback from Jove Books

And now here's a special excerpt from this
thrilling new series . . .

Jackson County, Missouri, 1862

As Seth Coulter lay his pocket watch on the bedside table and blew out the lantern, he thought he saw a light outside. Walking over to the window, he pulled the curtain aside to stare out into the darkness.

On the bed alongside him the mattress creaked, and his wife, Irma, raised herself on her elbows.

"What is it, Seth?" Irma asked. "What are you lookin' at?"

"Nothin', I reckon."

"Well, you're lookin' at somethin'."

"Thought I seen a light out there, is all."

Seth continued to look through the window for a moment longer. He saw only the moon-silvered West Missouri hills.

"A light? What on earth could that be at this time of night?" Irma asked.

"Ah, don't worry about it," Seth replied, still looking through the window. "It's prob'ly just lightning bugs."

"Lightning bugs? Never heard of lightning bugs this early in the year."

"Well, it's been a warm spring," Seth explained. Finally, he came away from the window, projecting to his wife an easiness he didn't feel. "I'm sure it's nothing," he said.

"I reckon you're right," the woman agreed. "Wisht the boys was here, though."

Seth climbed into bed. He thought of the shotgun over the fireplace mantle in the living room, and he wondered if he should go get it. He considered it for a moment, then decided against it. It would only cause Irma to ask questions, and just because he was feeling uneasy, was no reason to cause her any worry. He turned to her and smiled.

"What do you want the boys here for?" he asked. "If the boys was here, we couldn't be doin' this." Gently, he began pulling at her nightgown.

"Seth, you old fool, what do you think you're doin'?" Irma scolded. But there was a lilt of laughter in her voice, and it was husky, evidence that far from being put off by him, she welcomed his advances.

Now, any uneasiness Seth may have felt fell away as he tugged at her nightgown. Finally she sighed.

"You better let me do it," she said. "Clumsy as you are, you'll like-as-not tear it."

Irma pulled the nightgown over her head, then dropped it onto the floor beside her bed. She was forty-six years old, but a lifetime of hard work had kept her body trim, and she was proud of the fact that she was as firm now as she had been when she was twenty. She lay back on the bed and smiled up at her husband, her skin glowing silver in the splash of moonlight. Seth ran his hand down her nakedness, and she trembled under his touch. He marvelled that, after so many years of marriage, she could still be so easily aroused.

Three hundred yards away from the house, Emil Slaughter, leader of a band of Jayhawkers, twisted around in his saddle to look back at the dozen or so riders with him. Their faces were fired orange in the flickering lights of the torches. Felt hats were pulled low, and they were all wearing long dusters, hanging open to provide access to the pistols which protruded from their belts. His band of followers looked, Slaughter thought, as if a fissure in the earth had suddenly opened to allow a legion of demons to escape from hell. There was about them a hint of sulphur.

A hint of sulphur. Slaughter smiled at the thought. He liked that idea. Such an illusion would strike fear into the hearts of his victims, and the more frightened they were, the easier it would be for him to do his job.

Quickly, Slaughter began assigning tasks to his men.

"You two hit the smokehouse, take ever' bit of meat they got a'curin'."

"Hope they got a couple slabs of bacon," someone said.

"I'd like a ham or two," another put in.

"You three, go into the house. Clean out the pantry—flour, cornmeal, sugar, anything they got in there. And if you see anything valuable in the house, take it too."

"What about the people inside?"

"Kill 'em," Slaughter said succinctly.

"Women, too?"

"Kill 'em all."

"What about their livestock?"

"If they got 'ny ridin' horses, we'll take 'em. The plowin' animals, we'll let burn when we torch the barn. All right, let's go."

In the bedroom Seth and Irma were oblivious to what was going on outside. Seth was over her, driving himself into her moist triangle. Irma's breathing was coming faster and more shallow as Seth gripped her buttocks with his hands, pulling her up to meet him. He could feel her fingers digging into his shoulders, and see her jiggling, sweat-pearled breasts as her head flopped from side to side with the pleasure she was feeling.

Suddenly Seth was aware of a wavering, golden glow on the walls of the bedroom. A bright light was coming through the window.

"What the hell?" he asked, interrupting the rhythm and

holding himself up from her on stiffened arms, one hand on each side of her head.

"No, no," Irma said through clenched teeth. "Don't stop now, don't . . ."

"Irma, my God! The barn's on fire!" Seth shouted, as he disengaged himself.

"What?" Irma asked, now also aware of the orange glow in the room.

Seth got out of bed and started quickly, to pull on his trousers. Suddenly there was a crashing sound from the front of the house as the door was smashed open.

"Seth!" Irma screamed.

Drawing up his trousers, Seth started toward the living room and the shotgun he had over the fireplace.

"You lookin' for this, you Missouri bastard?" someone asked. He was holding Seth's shotgun.

"Who the hell are . . ." That was as far as Seth got. His question was cut off by the roar of the shotgun as a charge of double-aught buckshot slammed him back against the wall. He slid down to the floor, staining the wall behind him with blood and guts from the gaping exit wounds in his back.

"Seth! My God, no!" Irma shouted, running into the living room when she head the shotgun blast. So concerned was she about her husband that she didn't bother to put on her nightgown.

"Well, now, lookie what we got here," a beady-eyed Jayhawker said, staring at Irma's nakedness. "Boys, I'm goin' to have me some fun."

"No," Irma said, shaking now, not only in fear for her own life, but in shock from seeing her husband's lifeless body leaning against the wall.

Beady Eyes reached for Irma.

"Please," Irma whimpered. She twisted away from him. "Please."

"Listen to her beggin' me for it, boys. Lookit them titties! Damn, she's not a bad-lookin' woman, you know that?" His dark beady eyes glistened, rat-like, as he opened his pants then reached down to grab himself. His erection projected forward like a club.

"No, please, don't do this," Irma pleaded.

"You wait 'til I stick this cock in you, honey," Beady Eyes said. "Hell, you goin' to like it so much you'll think you ain't never been screwed before."

Irma turned and ran into the bedroom. The others followed her, laughing, until she was forced against the bed.

"Lookit this, boys! She's brought me right to her bed! You think this bitch ain't a'wantin' it?"

"I beg of you, if you've any kindness in you..." Irma started, but her plea was interrupted when Beady Eyes back-handed her so savagely that she fell across the bed, her mouth filled with blood.

"Shut up!" he said, harshly. "I don't like my women talkin' while I'm diddlin' 'em!"

Beady Eyes came down onto the bed on top of her, then he spread her legs and forced himself roughly into her. Irma felt as if she were taking a hot poker inside her, and she cried out in pain.

"Listen to her squealin'. He's really givin' it to her," one of the observers said.

Beady Eyes wheezed and gasped as he thrust into her roughly.

"Don't wear it out none," one of the others giggled. "We'uns want our turn!"

At the beginning of his orgasm, Beady Eyes enhanced his pleasure by one extra move that was unobserved by the others. Immediately thereafter he felt the convulsive tremors of the woman beneath him, and that was all it took to trigger his final release. He surrendered himself to the sensation of fluid and energy rushing out of his body, while he groaned and twitched in orgiastic gratification.

"Look at that! He's comin' in the bitch right now!" one of the others said excitedly. "Damn! You wait 'til I get in there! I'm going to come in quarts!"

Beady Eyes lay still on top of her until he had spent his final twitch, then he got up. She was bleeding from a stab wound just below her left breast.

"My turn," one of the others said, already taking out his cock. He had just started toward her when he saw the wound in the woman's chest, and the flat look of her dead eyes. "What the hell?" he asked. "What happened to her?"

The second man looked over at Beady Eyes in confusion. Then he saw Beady Eyes wiping blood off the blade of his knife.

"You son of bitch!" he screamed in anger. "You kilt her!"

"Slaughter told us to kill her," Beady Eyes replied easily.

"Well, you could'a waited 'til someone else got a chance to do her before you did it, you bastard!" The second man, putting himself back into his pants, started toward Beady Eyes when, suddenly, there was the thunder of a loud pistol shot.

"What the hell is going on in here?" Slaughter yelled. He was standing just inside the bedroom door, holding a smoking pistol in his hand, glaring angrily at them.

"This son of a bitch kilt the woman while he was doin' her!"

"We didn't come here to screw," Slaughter growled. "We come here to get supplies."

"But he kilt her *while* he was screwin' her! Who would do somethin' like that?"

"Before, during, after, what difference does it make?" Slaughter asked. "As long as she's dead. Now, you've got work to do, so get out there in the pantry, like I told you, and start gatherin' up what you can. You," he said to Beady Eyes, "go through the house, take anything you think we can sell. I want to be out of here in no more'n five minutes."

"Emil, what woulda been the harm in us havin' our turn?"

Slaughter cocked the pistol and pointed it at the one who was still complaining. "The harm is, I told you not to," he said. "Now, do you want to debate the issue?"

"No, no!" the man said quickly, holding his hands out toward Slaughter. "Didn't mean nothin' by it. I was just talkin', that's all."

"Good," Slaughter said. He looked over at Beady Eyes. "And you. If you ever pull your cock out again without me sayin' it's all right, I'll cut the goddamned thing off."

"It wasn't like you think, Emil," Beady Eyes said. "I was just tryin' to be easy on the woman, is all. I figured it would be better if she didn't know it was about to happen."

Slaughter shook his head. "You're one strange son of a bitch, you know that?" He stared at the three men for a minute, then he shook his head in disgust as he put his pistol back into his belt. "Get to work."

Beady Eyes was the last one out and as he started to leave he saw, lying on the chifferobe, a gold pocket watch. He glanced around to make sure no one was looking. Quickly, and unobserved, he slipped the gold watch into his own pocket.

This was a direct violation of Slaughter's standing orders. Anything of value found on any of their raids was to be divided equally among the whole. That meant that, by rights, he should give the watch to Slaughter, who would then sell it and divide whatever money it brought. But because it was loot, they would be limited as to where they could sell the watch. That meant it would bring much less than it was worth and by the time it was split up into twelve parts, each individual part would be minuscule. Better, by far, that he keep the watch for himself.

Feeling the weight of the watch riding comfortably in his pocket, he went into the pantry to start clearing it out.

"Lookie here!" the other mand detailed for the pantry said. "This here family ate pretty damn good, I'll tell you. We've made us quite a haul: flour, coffee, sugar, onions, potatoes, beans, peas, dried peppers."

"Yeah, if they's as lucky in the smokehouse, we're goin' to feast tonight!"

The one gathering the loot came into the pantry then, holding a bulging sack. "I found some nice gold candlesticks here, too," he said. "We ought to get somethin' for them."

"You men inside! Let's go!" Slaughter's shout came to them.

The Jayhawkers in the house ran outside where Slaughter had brought everyone together. Here, they were illuminated by the flames of the already-burning barn. Two among the bunch were holding flaming torches, and they looked at Slaughter expectantly.

With a nod of his head, Slaughter said, "All right, burn the rest of the buildings now."

Watch for

**LONGARM AND THE DOUBLE-BARREL
BLOWOUT**

223rd novel in the exciting LONGARM series
from Jove

Coming in July!

LONGARM

Explore the exciting Old West with one of the men who made it wild!

_LONGARM AND THE DEADLY THAW #198	0-515-11634-3/$3.99
_LONGARM AND THE UNWRITTEN LAW (GIANT #15)	0-515-11680-7/$4.99
_LONGARM AND THE BIG FIFTY #211	0-515-11895-8/$4.99
_LONGARM AND THE LUSTY LADY (GIANT #16)	0-515-11923-7/$5.50
_LONGARM AND THE MINUTE MEN #213	0-515-11942-3/$4.99
_LONGARM AND THE RACY LADIES #214	0-515-11956-3/$4.99
_LONGARM AND THE WHISKEY WOMAN #217	0-515-11998-9/$4.99
_LONGARM AND THE BOARDINGHOUSE WIDOW #218	0-515-12016-2/$4.99
_LONGARM AND THE CRYING CORPSE #219	0-515-12031-6/$4.99
_LONGARM AND THE INDIAN WAR #220	0-515-12050-2/$4.99
_LONGARM AND THE DEAD MAN'S REWARD #221	0-515-12069-3/$4.99
_LONGARM AND THE BACKWOODS BARONESS #222	0-515-12080-4/$4.99
_LONGARM AND THE DOUBLE-BARREL BLOWOUT #223 (7/97)	0-515-12104-5/$4.99

Payable in U.S. funds. No cash accepted. Postage & handling: $1.75 for one book, 75¢ for each additional. Maximum postage $5.50. Prices, postage and handling charges may change without notice. Visa, Amex, MasterCard call 1-800-788-6262, ext. 1, or fax 1-201-933-2316; refer to ad #201g

Or, check above books and send this order form to:	Bill my: ☐ Visa ☐ MasterCard ☐ Amex _____ (expires)
The Berkley Publishing Group	Card# _____
P.O. Box 12289, Dept. B	Daytime Phone # _____ ($10 minimum)
Newark, NJ 07101-5289	Signature _____

Please allow 4-6 weeks for delivery.   **Or enclosed is my:** ☐ check ☐ money order
Foreign and Canadian delivery 8-12 weeks.

Ship to:

Name_____	Book Total	$_____
Address_____	Applicable Sales Tax (NY, NJ, PA, CA, GST Can.)	$_____
City_____	Postage & Handling	$_____
State/ZIP_____	Total Amount Due	$_____

Bill to: Name_____

Address_____City_____
State/ZIP_____

First in an all-new series from the creators of Longarm!

BUSHWHACKERS

They were the most brutal gang of cutthroats ever
assembled. And during the Civil War, they sought justice
outside of the law—paying back every Yankee raid with one
of their own. They rode hard, shot straight, and had their
way with every willin' woman west of the Mississippi. No
man could stop them. No woman could resist them. And no
Yankee stood a chance of living when Quantrill's Raiders
rode into town...

Win and Joe Coulter become the two most wanted men in
the West. And they learn just how sweet—and deadly—
revenge could be...

Coming in July 1997
BUSHWHACKERS by B. J. Lanagan
0-515-12102-9/$5.99
Look for the second book in September 1997
BUSHWHACKERS #2: REBEL COUNTY
also by B. J. Lanagan 0-515-12142-8/$4.99

VISIT THE PUTNAM BERKLEY BOOKSTORE CAFÉ ON THE INTERNET:
http://www.berkley.com

Payable in U.S. funds. No cash accepted. Postage & handling: $1.75 for one book, 75¢ for each
additional. Maximum postage $5.50. Prices, postage and handling charges may change without
notice. Visa, Amex, MasterCard call 1-800-788-6262, ext. 1, or fax 1-201-933-2316; refer to ad #705

Or, check above books and send this order form to:	Bill my: ☐ Visa ☐ MasterCard ☐ Amex _____ (expires)
The Berkley Publishing Group	Card#_____
P.O. Box 12289, Dept. B	Daytime Phone #_____ ($10 minimum)
Newark, NJ 07101-5289	Signature_____
Please allow 4-6 weeks for delivery.	**Or enclosed is my:** ☐ check ☐ money order
Foreign and Canadian delivery 8-12 weeks.	

Ship to:

Name_____	Book Total	$_____
Address_____	Applicable Sales Tax (NY, NJ, PA, CA, GST Can.)	$_____
City_____	Postage & Handling	$_____
State/ZIP_____	Total Amount Due	$_____

Bill to: Name_____

Address_____ City_____

State/ZIP_____

A special offer for people who enjoy reading the best Westerns published today.

If you enjoyed this book, subscribe now and get...

TWO FREE WESTERNS

A $7.00 VALUE—NO OBLIGATION

If you would like to read more of the very best, most exciting, adventurous, action-packed Westerns being published today, you'll want to subscribe to True Value's Western Home Subscription Service.

TWO FREE BOOKS

When you subscribe, we'll send you your first month's shipment of the newest and best 6 Westerns for you to preview. With your first shipment, two of these books will be yours as our introductory gift to you absolutely *FREE* (a $7.00 value), regardless of what you decide to do.

Special Subscriber Savings

When you become a True Value subscriber you'll save money several ways. First, all regular

monthly selections will be billed at the low subscriber price of just $2.75 each. That's at least a savings of $4.50 each month below the publishers price. Second, there is never any shipping, handling or other hidden charges— *Free home delivery*. What's more there is no minimum number of books you must buy, you may return any selection for full credit and you can cancel your subscription at any time. A TRUE VALUE!

Mail the coupon below

To start your subscription and receive 2 FREE WESTERNS, fill out the coupon below and mail it today. We'll send your first shipment which includes 2 FREE BOOKS as soon as we receive it.

- -

Mail To: **True Value Home Subscription Services, Inc. P.O. Box 5235**
120 Brighton Road, Clifton, New Jersey 07015-5235

YES! I want to start reviewing the very best Westerns being published today. Send me my first shipment of 6 Westerns for me to preview FREE for 10 days. If I decide to keep them, I'll pay for just 4 of the books at the low subscriber price of $2.75 each; a total $11.00 (a $21.00 value). Then each month I'll receive the 6 newest and best Westerns to preview Free for 10 days. If I'm not satisfied I may return them within 10 days and owe nothing. Otherwise I'll be billed at the special low subscriber rate of $2.75 each; a total of $16.50 (at least a $21.00 value) and save $4.50 off the publishers price. There are never any shipping, handling or other hidden charges. I understand I am under no obligation to purchase any number of books and I can cancel my subscription at any time, no questions asked. In any case the 2 FREE books are mine to keep.

Name _____

Street Address _____ Apt. No. _____

City _____ State _____ Zip Code _____

Telephone _____ Signature _____

Terms and prices subject to change. Orders subject to acceptance by True Value Home Subscription Services, Inc.

(if under 18 parent or guardian must sign)

12080-4